The Case of the Christmas Diamond

The Candy Cane Mysteries, Volume 1

Peter Sullivan

Published by Peter Sullivan, 2023.

This is a work of fiction. Similarities to real people, places, or events are entirely coincidental.

THE CASE OF THE CHRISTMAS DIAMOND

First edition. November 15, 2023.

Copyright © 2023 Peter Sullivan.

ISBN: 979-8223360384

Written by Peter Sullivan.

For Marilyn and Parker, thank you for your love.

For Jeff and Barry, thank you for your support.

CHAPTER ONE

Candace "Andy" Kayne enjoyed the drive.

The prospect of a six-hour car ride would intimidate many people. But not Andy. She was enjoying her journey from the Bay Area of San Francisco to the snow-capped mountains of Tahoe. The serene solitude was refreshing. Just forty-eight hours ago, she was working in the coffee shop, slinging cappuccinos for bohemian yuppies.

That was when she got a surprising call from her long-time friend, Olivia. There wasn't much a bohemian bookworm like Andy had in common with the likes of Olivia Kenilworth. Being the daughter of the late industrialist Frederick Kenilworth, Olivia was regarded as Beverly Hills royalty. It was pure luck that, as a little girl, Olivia's parents had decided she and her brother Liam needed to "rough it" and chose the summer camp in Maine where Andy's parents worked. The two girls had become inseparable. First for the entire summer, and later, many summers thereafter.

Now, all these years later, Andy was alone in her car, on her way to attend her first Annual Kenilworth Christmas Gathering. The snow dusted hills and limitless almond groves of Northern California were a far cry from the hustle and bustle of the Embarcadero. From the coffee shop where she worked. Being one of those national chains where every recipe was dictated by corporate fiat, Andy found the job lacking in creative freedom. Her only artistic outlet was devising gimmicks for the tip jar. Put a dollar in the left jar if you prefer Agatha Christie, or the right if you prefer Jackie Evenson.

Jackie Evenson. If Agatha Christie had mastered the stuffy British drawing room mystery, Jackie had done the same for the United States. Replacing the European intellectual bravado of Hercule Poirot with the genteel Southern charms of Birdie Pickett, Jackie consistently ranked in the top ten authors of popular American fiction. Peruse the shelves of any bookstore and you'd find cloned dinosaurs terrorizing theme parks, demonic house cats resurrected from their pet cemeteries, and...the cozy crimes of Jackie Evenson.

And she was Andy's favorite.

In fact, Andy downloaded a vast selection of her audio books for the car ride. She'd been so busy lately, with her *own* attempted foray into mystery fiction that she'd missed the release of the latest Birdie Pickett mystery *Murder and Mimosas.*

The drive would be the perfect time to catch up. She was even more excited because Jackie herself narrated the audio book. She could spend the entire journey with her favorite character, guided by the voice of her favorite author. Instead of the monotony of the flat California farmland, Andy found her imagination drifting to a restaurant in Georgia.

Birdie Pickett marched down the aisle, under the watchful eyes of the nervous patrons.

"Two dead bodies," Birdie said in a soothing Southern accent that felt like Miss Marple meets Mississippi. "No one else has come in. And no one has gone out."

Birdie continued pacing as a server, Josie, refilled the champagne flutes.

"On the one hand, we have the wealthy and deceased Mr. Barron. On the other, a bartender, Scott. A college student whose promising future was cut short because he was in the wrong place at the wrong time. The

question is: which one of our dinner companions sought to complement their brunch... with a side order of murder?"

She stopped. Her eyes searched each of the guests.

"Was it the envious wife, having recently learned that her husband was spending late nights in the company of his beautiful new assistant? Or the bitter partner, driven into a jealous rage at the thought of losing a valuable patent?"

Each of the suspects' eyes averted her gaze. Were they uncomfortable being singled out? Or was it guilt?

Listening to the mystery helped pass the time for Andy. Now that the story was almost over, she was confident she had it solved. It was one reason she loved Jackie Evenson's writings. Unlike many of her contemporaries, her stories were what readers would call "fair play mysteries." They gave the reader everything they needed to solve the case on their own.

And now, listening to the tale over her car's old stereo, Andy believed she had. *What if,* she thought to herself, *Mr. Barron wasn't the target after all? What if it was the bartender?*

She listened closely as the story continued, eager to see if her conclusion was correct.

Birdie took her place at the head of the room. It was time to reveal the culprit.

"We've been so fixed on Mr. Barron," she said, "the man with everything to lose and companions with everything to gain, we've failed to ask the obvious question. What if it wasn't our bartender who was in the wrong place at the wrong time, but the executive who was the collateral damage?"

Andy grinned upon hearing this. *She was right!*

Birdie spun on her heels to face the waitress, Josie. "You must have blown a gasket! After dedicating twenty years of sweat and tears to this establishment, Craig would dare leave the restaurant to Scott instead of you?!"

"That's absurd!" Josie exclaimed.

Birdie wasn't deterred. "Absurd enough to kill him over it?"

"You watched as Scott went into the wine cellar for Mr. Barron's special order, the expensive vintage he preferred," Birdie continued, running through the morning's events in her head. "You knew they kept that bottle on the top shelf in the cellar. Just like you knew Craig would send Scott to retrieve it. All you had to do was wait. Little did you realize that Mr. Barron, a noted wine connoisseur, would have asked to see the cellar for himself."

"That cellar is unlocked during business hours," Josie protested. "Anyone could have gone down there!"

"You are correct," Birdie acknowledged. "That is... anyone who'd spent their lunch break at the local park, as you say you did that day."

Sure enough, Birdie continued her account of the incident. "How else do you explain the presence of white mason sand? Which, I might point out, is not native to this area but imported. And used exclusively for park landscaping?"

Growing nervous, Josie again tried to deflect Birdie's accusation. "You're reaching," she stammered. "It's a public park!"

"No, madam, it is you who reached," Birdie astutely observed. "When you picked up the gun shells."

Birdie held up her phone, revealing a photo she'd taken of the crime scene in the cellar. "On a hot day, at temperatures like this, the oil and solids in your lunch would have separated, making quite a mess. You really should have washed your hands before you committed the crime as well."

Josie realized she'd been caught. Not red handed, but sand handed. The walls of justice would move in soon. Her window for escape was rapidly closing. She did what any guilty party might have done. She ran for the exit.

The police, however, were waiting, handcuffs in hand. She was grabbed, her hands thrust behind her back. She felt the cold metal against *her wrist and the halting snap of the locking mechanism. Resigned to her fate, she didn't resist as the officers led her out of the room.*

"And that..." Birdie said with that trademark twinkle in her eye, "is how we do things back in bayou country."

"In a quarter of a mile, make a U turn," the GPS application commanded in its disarmingly placid tone.

That was when Andy realized that she'd been so wrapped up in the story, she'd missed her turn!

"Great," she muttered, pulling the steering wheel into a U turn.

"This has been "Mimosas & Murder" by Jackie Evenson." An announcer called out from her car radio, "Read by the author."

Turning off the main road, Andy wound her way up the twisting mountain road above Tahoe. The higher she got, the deeper the snow grew. She started to worry. She hadn't gotten the proper chains for her tires. What if an overzealous highway patrolman made her turn around? However, such interference never came. Andy went higher into the mountains. There, her older car, which had seen better days, felt out of place amidst the big money estates. Even its lone bumper sticker, the one which proudly advertised "Camp Horizons" in Ogunquit, Maine, was peeling.

It was immediately clear to the young woman that she'd left her usual world behind. The world she was stepping into would be one of privilege and influence: two things which Andy had spent her life being blissfully ignorant of.

She had arrived at the Kenilworth lodge.

IT WAS NO ACCIDENT that Lake Tahoe was called the Jewel of the Sierra. What Mark Twain once referred to as "the fairest picture the whole earth affords" was now the home of some of the state's wealthiest families. Surrounded by snow-capped alpine mountains, their gated mountainside estates sat nestled within lush pine forests. No wonder the Kenilworths had built their winter lodge here, overlooking the gleaming sapphire-colored lake below. This was the dominion of Californian aristocracy.

"Whoa," Andy exclaimed, as she approached the imposing iron gate. With the indomitable barricade towering over her tiny car, she was both impressed and intimidated. She felt a bit like Dorothy, having reached the end of the yellow brick road, and imagined the gates of the Emerald City swinging open as this gate did, on its own. *Someone,* she realized, *had been watching.* She wondered how long they'd been spying on her and figured it had probably been from the very moment she'd turned off the main road. With such a lavish property, Andy should have expected personal privacy would take a backseat to security.

She pulled the car up the long driveway, watching through her rear-view mirror as the large gate swing shut behind her. At that moment, she wondered. Was this barrier intended to lock out the outside world? *Or lock her in?*

Perched high in the Sierra Nevada Mountains, the Kenilworth winter estate stood as a testament to luxury and sophistication. The lodge's ruggedly opulent turrets and peaks were adorned with enough Christmas decorations to rival the north pole itself. And yet, as Andy pulled up the circular driveway, she spotted a man hanging even *more* lights. Based on his sweater and khaki pants, she guessed he must have been a resident or guest.

As Andy climbed out of her car, feeling the crisp winter air on her cheeks, she grew nervous. She knew how her host's mother felt about her and that she'd be judged by every word and action. She'd brought a potted poinsettia as a gift. Now it felt woefully inadequate.

"Margaret, thank you so much for inviting me," she rehearsed, trying to find the right words for the inevitable encounter. "Margaret, it's so good to see you..."

Margaret, she thought to herself, *was far too informal.* This woman would never want to be addressed in such a casual manner. *Mrs.*

Kenilworth, she decided, *would be the proper way.* "Olivia told me your Christmas parties were legendary."

Finally she just gave up. "I should've booked an Airbnb," she grumbles with a sigh. But then, she got the sensation that someone was watching her. Could someone have been watching from the vast woods beyond the perimeter? She felt the hairs on the back of her neck stand up. Coming from the bustling metropolis of San Francisco, she found the silence of the wilderness unnerving.

"Candace Kayne!"

She spun to see Olivia Kenilworth, her best friend. She was right, someone had been watching her! Luckily, it was a friendly face. Unlike Andy, Olivia was impeccably preppy in every way, and, instead of a beater, she climbed out of a lavish, black town car.

"Olivia!" Andy replied, relieved to see her dear friend.

"Inside would be great," Olivia motioned to her driver before pulling her friend into a hug.

"You didn't have any trouble finding the place, did you?" Olivia asked warmly.

"The GPS got a little funky the last mile or so," Andy replied, neglecting to mention her distraction with the audiobook.

Olivia just laughed, understandingly. "I should've warned you," she admitted. "The signals aren't great up here."

With Olivia's things already inside, Andy went to retrieve her own luggage.

"What are you doing?" Olivia exclaimed. "I'll get the butler." She then turned to the butler standing at the door. She was a thin, humorless woman named Bridgette. Everything about her was severe, from her humorless demeanor to her hair, which was pulled back tight. It surprised Andy that the butler was a woman. She'd learned about household staff only from watching television, and usually period programs at that.

"You're a guest!" Olivia motioned to Bridgette, who clapped her hands. A Valet emerged from the house and retrieved Andy's luggage.

"So," Andy said, watching her luggage being whisked away. "This is my bestie's *famous* winter lodge?"

"Winter *retreat*, mother calls it," Olivia clarified with a self-effacing grin. "The woman drives five miles into the mountain and calls it roughing it."

"Oh yeah," Andy laughed. "Super quaint."

Then, Olivia, letting down her guard, opened up. "I'm just happy you're here to rescue me from my family."

"It's not like you gave me a choice."

"What was I supposed to do?" Olivia asked. "Let my best friend spend Christmas in her apartment alone? Binging audio books and eating Chinese takeout?"

But that really *was* how Andy had expected to spend the holidays. Only now, hearing it from Olivia's mouth, did she realize how pathetic it sounded. Still, it was *her* time: a treasured moment of solace that was hers and hers alone.

"Maybe I *enjoy* spending Christmas with General Tso," Andy shrugged.

Olivia just shook her head. Her friend *must* have been kidding. As they approached the house, they passed under the man hanging lights on his ladder.

"That's Uncle Gary," Olivia gestured. "He loves three things. Money, family and Christmas. Specifically, in that order."

"Looking good, Gary!" Olivia exclaimed before escorting Andy inside.

Her tour of the Kenilworth estate had just begun.

AS THE ENORMOUS FRONT doors swung open and Andy took her first steps into the lodge, clutching her potted poinsettia, she felt overwhelmed. The vaulted ceilings and exposed wooden beams of the foyer had been decorated with fresh pine garland, twinkling fairy lights, and enormous red velvet bows. A staff of skilled decorators meticulously wrapped the banister with lights. Andy watched as they adjusted the last bauble and sighed in satisfaction.

An advent calendar, meticulously crafted to resemble the lodge itself, revealed the date as December 22nd. Where had the month gone? Where did *the year* go?

"Mother has a whole itinerary," Olivia said, explaining how the Annual Kenilworth Christmas Gathering would unfold. "Game night tonight, spiced ale tomorrow on Tibb's Eve, dinner on Christmas Eve, and finally, the big soiree Christmas day."

"Game night?" Andy asked.

Olivia just shot her a knowing smile. "If you liked my family before, wait 'till you see how competitive they can get!"

"To be honest, I'm surprised she even agreed to let me stay," Andy said. Olivia's mother would not have welcomed her without some debate. *Perhaps even an argument would have been necessary*, she thought. However, the look on Olivia's face said it all. There had been no conversation because, as Andy now realized, *Margaret was unaware that Andy was invited to stay!*

"How could you not tell her?" Andy gasped to her friend.

"There's more than enough rooms!" Olivia insisted, perhaps rehearsing for what she'd planned to tell her mother in their inevitable showdown.

"She looks down on me!"

"She's a Kenilworth. We look down on everyone. Bunch of spoiled babies!" Olivia scoffed as she began rifling through their mail. Even though she hadn't lived at the address for years and had long stopped getting mail there, she always checked. Alas, the daily batch was comprised of junk mailers, Christmas cards, and a letter from a genealogy company addressed to her brother Liam.

"Take my brother Liam." Olivia observed. "Thirty years old and *still* having his mail sent to mommy's house."

Andy laughed, but Olivia could tell she was still nervous. She instinctually recognized that her friend just needed some reassurance. "Don't worry," she gently comforted her friend. "They're going to love you."

"Who said I was worried?" Andy said, breaking eye contact to look away.

"Aha!" Olivia exclaimed, recognizing the tell. It was something she'd always observed. Even as far back as summer camp, whenever Andy lied, *she always broke eye contact.*

"You always look away when you lie!" Olivia explained.

"I do not!" Andy protested, before looking away a second time.

"You just did it again!"

"Fine, maybe I do," Andy admitted, "But as long as your family's game isn't poker, I should be fine."

Next on the tour came the kitchen. The culinary haven boasted top-of-the-line stainless steel appliances, marble countertops, a stylish breakfast nook, and a massive island complete with contemporary bar stools. It was, naturally, large enough to feed a small restaurant. But Andy couldn't shake the notion that most of it was probably going to waste. The idea of someone such as Margaret Kenilworth slaving over a hot stove struck her as comically naïve. Of course, that didn't mean she wouldn't have the latest and trendiest appliances, such as the imported Italian espresso machine currently sitting on the counter, a red bow still affixed to its face.

"A Christmas present to my mother from Uncle Gary," Olivia noted, showing off the coffee maker with pride. "As if the woman has ever made a cup of coffee in her life."

As expected of an event such as this, someone *else* was doing the cooking. She vaguely remembered her friend Olivia mentioning something about a "Michelin award-winning chef." While Andy was, admittedly, as far from a foodie as you could get, even *she* could acknowledge how delicious it all smelled. There, on the stove, stewed a soup more invitingly rich and creamy than she'd ever seen. It was *so* enticing that she instinctually reached for a spoon and moved in for a taste. Which was when she felt an icy blade against her throat.

Someone *didn't want their soup touched.*

"If you value your life," barked the French-accented voice, "you'll back away from my vichyssoise!"

Olivia turned to see the chef, Raphael. Even though he couldn't have been a year or two older than she, he'd definitely spent a few years toiling in the trenches. As expected from a modern trendy chef, his arms were both covered in sleeves of tattoos. It would seem that food was not his only vice. Then, he broke out in a wide, gregarious grin.

"This is my friend, Candace," Olivia said, introducing the two.

"Please." Andy said, never wanting to use her first name, "Just *Andy.*"

"She'll be spending Christmas with us," her friend explained to the chef.

"A guest!" the gregarious French chef exclaimed, dipping a large ladle into his pot of creamy goodness. "In that case, why settle for a taste when you can have a whole mouthful?"

Andy sampled the soup and found it even more delicious than she'd expected.

"She was actually wondering if you can make General Tso's chicken," Olivia laughed, much to Andy's embarrassment. She wondered what Olivia would have said had she known that Andy's dinner the previous night comprised ramen noodles and a fistful of Cheez Its.

"Olivia!" Andy exclaimed.

The chef was not as judgmental as Andy feared. "Mademoiselle," he said with that same wide smile, "I shall make you a chicken the General himself could only <u>dream</u> of!"

With that, the tour continued on.

"That espresso machine must have cost your uncle a fortune!" Andy exclaimed as the two women made their way into the hall.

"Gary just wants to show off," Olivia rolled her eyes. "Not that *anyone here* would know how to work it."

"I could," Andy offered. But Olivia wasn't about to let her guest work on her restful Christmas holiday.

"You're not here to work," she insisted. "You're here to relax! C'mon. I'll get you situated in your room."

At that moment, Andy, still distracted by the lavishness in which she found herself, bumped into someone! Not just anyone, but Olivia's older brother, Liam. Andy hadn't seen Liam since they were children, but he had that same, unmistakable boyish grin she'd recognize anywhere. Quickly searching for the right words to apologize, Andy found herself unexpectedly tongue tied. Now there was a *new* distraction for her to occupy herself with. At least she hadn't dropped her poinsettia.

"Watch it, you moron!" Liam yelled loudly. Suddenly, Andy's heart sank. Was one innocent, clumsy moment really worth such a harsh reaction? But as he reached down to retrieve the newspaper he'd dropped, opened to the sports section on which she saw certain scores circled with a pen, she realized that his exclamation was not directed at her. It had been a conversation he was having over his Bluetooth headset.

"No, no," he clarified, "I'm on the..."

"Oh! Right! Sorry." She felt silly about the misunderstanding. *Of course, he'd been on the phone*! However, as she knelt down to help pick up the paper, their eyes met for the first time. He suddenly forgot about his call altogether as he realized where he'd seen her before.

"Candace?"

She smiled, relieved that he hadn't forgotten her after all. However, she quickly corrected him, having not gone by *Candace* in a long time. "Andy."

"You remember Liam?" Olivia interjected, as if she felt uncomfortable by the clear attraction between her brother and best friend. "My *older brother from another mother*."

"Wow. You look…" Liam started, choosing his compliments wisely, "you've grown up."

"It happens."

"Andy is going to be spending Christmas with us!" Olivia said, still happy to have company, even if she wasn't completely at ease with sharing Andy with her older brother.

"I have to finish this," Liam motioned to the Bluetooth, "but, if you're going to be around, we should catch up!"

"Looking forward to it." Andy grinned.

With that, Liam walked away, resuming his phone conversation. Yet, he still shot a glance back over his shoulder at Andy. Along with a smile.

"Brother from another mother?" Andy turned to Olivia.

"When we were kids, no one believed we were *actually* related," Olivia explained. "Frankly, I still don't. But you're in luck. He just called off his engagement."

"That's too bad," was all Andy could manage at the moment, as if recognizing the awkwardness of the dynamic. "But I don't know if it's a good idea, you know… my best friend's brother and all…" She looked away, a fact Olivia quickly seized upon.

"You are such a liar!" she laughed. Andy realized that her little tell had revealed her genuine interest in Liam.

At that moment, a commanding female voice boomed from the top of the stairs. "No! No poinsettias!"

Andy looked up to see Margaret, Olivia and Liam's mother, a woman so severely intimidating that her very presence was enough to give Andy anxiety.

"I specifically told the clerk," Margaret continued, in the middle of a phone call, "This party needs to be unique!" That's when she noticed her daughter, standing there with Andy.

"Hold on," she interrupted her train of thought. "My daughter, whom I haven't seen in three months, just arrived from San Francisco."

Watching her mother put the call on hold, Olivia gave her a warm embrace, although Margaret didn't have a warm bone in her icy body.

"I asked for Christmas amaryllis, and they send a van full of poinsettias," the woman remarked in her typically haughty tone. "Does this look like a Michael's to you?"

Andy suddenly felt very self-conscious about that poinsettia she'd brought as a housewarming gift. She quickly stashed the red plant on a nearby table, alongside countless others just like it, hoping that Margaret hadn't noticed. If she *had*, she was at least polite enough not to mention it.

"Your diamond, ma'am." Andy heard an authoritative female voice call out in a stately British accent. It was Bridgette, the butler. She held up a very large jewelry box. As she opened it, Andy became overwhelmed with curiosity.

"*That's* a diamond?" Andy whispered to Olivia.

"Wait 'til you see it," her friend grumbled. "She loves it more than her two children."

"I had it cleaned for your party as requested," Bridgette continued in her posh accent, reaching to open the box. Andy had never seen a jewelry box of that size before, and knew that, whatever its contents were, it would certainly be worth a look. And it was.

The Christmas Diamond, as the family referred to it, had been in the family for generations. In fact, a painting of an earlier Kenilworth matriarch hung over the fireplace in the study, its comely subject wearing that *same piece* around her slender neck. The diamond was 170-carats and surrounded by rubies and emeralds. The red and green prism of color gave the piece the unmistakable color palette of the holiday. Margaret only wore it once a year, at her family's lavish holiday gathering.

"Thank you, Bridgette," Margaret said, taking back her necklace, still in its ornate box. Then, as if actually noticing Andy for the first time, turned to her daughter. "What's Candace doing here?"

"*Andy,*" Olivia corrected her mother, "is actually *staying with us.*"

Margaret was aghast. Andy's heart sank. Until now, she hadn't thought of her visit as an imposition.

"It's okay, really," she replied, "I can stay at the motel down the street."

"She isn't staying at a motel," Olivia insisted. "She's staying in our spare guest room."

Margaret gasped. "The guest room? Where I keep my collection of very-expensive, *very-rare*, imported German figurines?"

"Unless you'd like *me* to spend Christmas in the motel as well?"

Stalemate. Margaret knew her daughter wasn't bluffing. She had looked forward to this visit for some time and wasn't about to give up time with her only daughter.

"We'd be honored," she replied, through gritted teeth and a half smile.

"Love you, mother."

Margaret, however, couldn't resist stealing the last word and pulled her new guest aside. "Just so you know," she said quietly, "I *will* be watching you."

Andy nodded politely as Margaret turned back to her phone. "Are you still there? Good. I'd like you to connect me with someone who actually *has* taste."

Stealing one last look at Andy, the woman returned up the stairs, clutching that diamond box tightly.

THE LODGE'S BEDROOMS were luxurious sanctuaries with enormous windows framing the picturesque landscapes. Each had a private balcony or patio, and the ensuite bathrooms featured marble, deep soaking tubs, and rainfall showers.

The moment Andy set foot in the guest room; she understood why Margaret had been hesitant about her staying there. The antique curio cabinet, an exquisite piece of furniture itself, was the perfect place for Margaret's delicate collection of porcelain figurines. Its shelves had been lined with a plush, velvet material that cradled her sizable collection while simultaneously displaying them. Each of the figurines was intricately detailed, with every tiny fold of clothing, strand of hair, and flower petal meticulously hand-crafted by artisans.

Bordering upon obsession, it seemed everywhere Andy looked, the porcelain cherubs' frozen smiles just stared right back. It was unsettling. A young boy and girl stood side by side, in traditional Bavarian dress, laden with baskets of apples. Their rosy cheeks and gleaming eyes seemed to *come alive*, evoking the innocence and simplicity of childhood. Nearby, another pair of children stood, captured in a moment of mirth. The boy held a bright red umbrella aloft, while the girl sheltered beneath it. Their joyful expressions and the vibrant colors of their clothing radiated happiness not even a gentle rain shower could dampen.

There were more. A girl in a bonnet and apron held a basket of fluffy yellow chicks. A chimney sweep, his rosy, red cheeks speckled with soot, carried a long brush. A young musician played a flute, serenading a young girl, who clutched a dove in a sentimental depiction of enduring love and connection.

Bridgette and the household staff had already brought up Andy's bags, placing them neatly on the bed.

"Don't let mother get to you." Olivia tried to calm her down. "She has this whole confident, posh society woman act down. But it's just to hide how stressed she is."

Andy appreciated the effort. "I've got this. Go be with your family."

Olivia smiled and left. Andy started unpacking but she couldn't shake an unbearable curiosity about those figurines. *Could they really be so valuable?* She opened the cabinet and removed one for a closer look: a little drummer boy. Gazing into its face, she suddenly heard Bing Crosby's soothing voice, crooning a Christmas carol in her mind.

I am a poor boy too, pa-rum pum pum pum...

"You don't look *that* expensive," she remarked under her breath, as if undervaluing the inanimate child might make her feel better. *I have no gift to bring pa-rum pum pum pum... that's fit to give our King pa-rum pum...*

Suddenly, she heard a loud thump! She quickly shoved the figurine in her pocket! Hiding it! She couldn't risk anyone seeing it in her hand.

She pulled back the lace sheers which hung from the window. Her window overlooked a balcony and, beyond that, the vast property. Straining to look, Andy saw nothing except the pure, driven snow. *A white Christmas, indeed.* Suitably unsettled, she turned back to the room, neglecting to notice the unmistakable shadow wiping across the window behind her. *Someone was outside!*

After she unpacked, Andy grew curious about the lodge and what other secrets it might hold. She decided, with the time she had until dinner, she should investigate further. After all, with her wealthy host's unique eccentricities, she imagined the figurine collection was probably just the tip of the iceberg.

ANDY VENTURED BACK down the sweeping staircase leading into the foyer. She found herself back in that spacious rotunda and ventured in the direction that Olivia hadn't taken her, towards the very heart of the lodge: an impressive great room, with its high ceilings and massive timber purlins. An enormous stone fireplace rose from floor to ceiling, providing both warmth and a focal point for gathering. An old hunting rifle, specifically an original flintlock musket from 1816 and one of only 100 ever made, sat on display on the mantle. The furnishings were a blend of modern design and rustic charm, with touches of leather, fur, and wood accents. There were plush, oversized sofas and armchairs with sumptuous throws and cushions. Perfect for relaxing and taking in the breathtaking views of Mt. Tallac through the large panoramic windows. *There'd be plenty of time for that later,* Andy imagined.

A towering Christmas tree, bedecked in shimmering ornaments and golden ribbons, nearly brushed the ceiling. There sat a baby grand piano and ornate harp, both of which Andy surmised probably possessed rich histories of their own. She vaguely recalled Olivia mentioning that the piano had been played at a function for Abraham Lincoln at one point.

For entertainment, they equipped the lodge with a state-of-the-art home theater, complete with a massive flat-screen TV, reclining leather seats, and a surround sound system. Next to it, a well-stocked game room featured a pool table, a shuffleboard, and a bar area stocked with fine wines and spirits.

She then turned her attention to the home office, or as a one percenter might call it, *the study.* Stepping through the door from the hall, she entered a wood-paneled transitional hallway, a dark oak-lined path leading into the studious inner sanctum. Indeed, it was baroque, its high ceilings lined with clothbound volumes of first edition literature. It all felt meticulously staged, as if no one had actually taken advantage of the remarkable tomes.

"*Pardon moi,*" Andy laughed to herself, imagining herself the heroine in her own, period gothic romance novel, "*but where might a lady find the loo?*"

Besides an ornate desk sat an assortment of old framed family photos, some of which had long yellowed. There was also a collection of antique typewriters, the sheer volume of which seemed second only to Margaret's figurine collection. Most notably, however, was the odd wood panel in the side of the shelf. It seemed to hide something and, as if her curiosity grabbed control of her limbs, Andy just had to reach out and touch it. The panel snapped open, revealing a large, built-in safe, and its impenetrable iron door.

"I'm sure there is a perfectly good explanation why you're in my study, Candace." Margaret snapped, having discovered her guest's uninvited, and apparently unwelcome, presence.

"I was looking for the loo... er, *bathroom*." Andy spun.

"Other direction."

A man Andy hadn't seen before then joined Margaret. Tall and imposing, he dressed in slacks and shirt and tie. As if the square jaw and icy stare hadn't said it all... the police badge clipped to his belt finished the sentence.

"My apologies," Andy uttered, slowly backing her way out.

"Wait," the Detective interrupted her with a wave of his hand.

Andy froze, suddenly remembering the figurine in her pocket! She'd forgotten to put it back! Her heart pounded as the Detective drew near. She quickly found her hand covering her pocket, trying to hide it from view as best as possible.

"Candace," Margaret coldly announced. "This is Detective Billings."

"Um, hi..." was the best she could muster in response, her mind restlessly mulling over the incriminating evidence bulging in her pocket.

"I've been watching you since the moment you pulled through my gate," Margaret said quietly, as if about to level an accusation.

"Is that right?"

"Oh, go easy on the poor girl," the Detective interjected with a disarming twinkle in his eye. "She has nothing to hide. Right?"

Andy could only smile and tried to defuse the tension she felt. "Well, there was this parking ticket I got a couple of months ago."

"Guess I can let that one slide," Detective Billings grinned until his face darkened, perhaps only in jest. "For now."

"I'll get out of your hair." Andy resumed her retreat. She was almost to the door when Detective Billings called out.

"And Andy?" He said. She turned nervously as he simply grinned. "See you around."

The relief hit her like a tidal wave. "I look forward to it."

With that, Andy raced out as fast as she could without risking further incrimination.

ONCE THE OTHER GUESTS arrived, it was like a hurricane blew through the quiet mansion. Valets helped the rest of the Kenilworth family unload their chauffeured SUVs, bloated with expensive luggage and professionally swathed Christmas gifts.

The manor's staff, adorned in their finest attire, buzzed with excitement. Bridgette, the butler, held a clipboard and a vision that rivaled even the most festive holiday fairy tales. The guests' gifts were all carefully and artfully stacked beneath the Christmas tree in the great room. Already adorned with its comfortable furniture and a warm, inviting ambiance, the room was being transformed into a winter wonderland. The twinkling lights, the shimmering ornaments, and the tantalizing scent of holiday treats filled the air with enchantment. A bounty of red, green and glitter, the growing mound of holiday treasure beneath the imposing pine felt like something out of a catalog: carefully designed and curated. That, of course, was the Kenilworth way. In this gilded world, appearance always trumped the heart.

A collection of nutcrackers, resplendent in their brightly colored uniforms, stood sentinel near the entrance. The aroma of holiday treats filled the air as a table, adorned with a red and green tablecloth and a sparkling centerpiece, was festooned with platters of gingerbread cookies, sugar cookies shaped like stars and bells, and chocolate truffles dusted with edible glitter. There was even a bowl of Christmas wassail, complete with large cinnamon sticks and a festive ladle. Nearby, a platter of delicate finger sandwiches, stuffed with cucumber and smoked salmon, awaited hungry guests.

Andy descended the stairs into the whirlwind of preparation that was taking place, bewildered and overwhelmed. She'd changed her clothes and was now wearing an appropriately tacky Christmas sweater. In sharp contrast to the shallow and impersonal holiday façade in which she found herself, this was a woman who actually felt a sense of Christmas spirit. Certainly, in opposition to the tailored cyclone currently barreling down the hallway: Olivia's uncle Gary, his tennis-preppy wife Leonora, and their college aged daughter Harper, with her beret and French flag pin. Coming from the home office, clearly something had not gone Gary's way.

"This is ridiculous!" Gary huffed, his feet stomping across the marble flooring. "We fly all the way across the country to make her a killer offer and my sister couldn't care less!"

"Heaven forbid someone actually says no to you for once, Daddy," Harper noted with one of her trademark eye rolls. However, as she reached for her ubiquitous cell phone, Olivia bounded over with a large red stocking. She held it open expectantly.

"No phones in the lodge during functions," she told the teen. "Mother's rules."

Harper protested with a groan and yet another eye roll.

"Harper." Her mother shot her a disapproving look. "We do it *every year*."

"And it's annoying *every year*," the girl shot back without missing a beat.

"We need to stay on your aunt's good side," her mother warned.

"My aunt isn't an influencer."

"And neither are you."

Game, set, match. Harper begrudgingly lowered her smart phone into Olivia's stocking. Her parents did the same without protest.

Andy watched the scene unfold with amusement. This cast of characters was far more interesting than the family gatherings she'd experienced as a child: where the only holiday drama came from rooting for opposite teams in that year's Aloha Bowl.

"I see you've found Aunt Leonora and her daughter Harper. My uncle Gary's family." Olivia observed, approaching Andy with her large stocking extended.

Andy eyed Harper, who, as if on cue, pulled out a second, back-up phone she'd hidden! "That apple didn't fall far from the tree."

"Newton's law at its finest." Olivia laughed.

"What's their story?" Andy asked.

"Sour grapes. Older sister inherits all the money, marries wealthy, while her younger brother fails at one venture after another." Then, regarding Andy's own phone, "Phone?"

"What are we supposed to do?" Andy asked her.

"Make conversation? Like the old days?"

With a laugh, noting the irony of Olivia's comment, Andy dropped her own phone in the bag. But that was when, hearing the slam of the large front door echoing through the lodge, she looked up.

A new guest had stepped inside. Judging from the relatively meager mix of luggage and Christmas gifts carried by the accompanying valet, this guest lived with a bit more humility than the others. In fact, this new arrival wasn't a Kenilworth at all. It took only a second for Olivia to recognize the kind and expressive face of the middle-aged African American woman who now strode in her direction. Her attire was more suited for a library than the self-important holiday soiree. Mystery writer Jackie Evenson had arrived.

"Wait, is that...?" the star-struck Andy asked Olivia. "Jackie Evenson? The writer?"

"She and my mother have been friends for years." Olivia observed with casual familiarity, Andy doubted her friend had even read one of Jackie's classic novels.

Gracious, Jackie could sense Andy's enthusiasm. She extended her hand. "I don't believe we've had the pleasure. And you are...?"

"A fan. Big fan." Andy exclaimed, her mouth running faster than she could even think. "Candace. Andy. Kayne."

Jackie's eyes narrowed mischievously. "<u>Candace</u> Kayne, huh? As in *Candy Cane...*?"

"Please," Andy replied, almost embarrassed by the moniker. "Just Andy."

"So, *just Andy.*" Jackie grinned before continuing. "Olivia's friend since... childhood? Formerly of New England? Here for Christmas, I imagine."

Andy couldn't believe her ears. Jackie Evenson knew who she was? "She's told you about me?"

"She didn't have to."

"Then *how* did you...?"

Olivia beamed, as if Jackie's legendary skills of deduction were, in true Kenilworth fashion, a parlor trick to be used to impress guests like Andy.

"You're the same age," Jackie notes, "and, as the only other non-Kenilworth here, I'm guessing the car with the summer camp bumper sticker out front belongs to you."

Andy brimmed with curiosity about how Jackie figured this out. "And New England?"

"If the likes of Olivia Kenilworth are attending, I suspect Camp Horizons is not inexpensive. In which case, one of your parents worked there, and *that* means you grew up within commuting distance." Then, without missing a beat, she dove into the small paper bag she carried by her side. "Christmas cookie?"

Andy grinned, digging into both the bag as well and her extensive knowledge of Jackie's bibliography. "There is no greater pleasure in life than..."

"... a well-made cookie." Jackie finished her quote, impressed. "You've read *Mayhem Molasses*!"

"Are you kidding?" Andy gushed, "That was your very first *Birdie Pickett mystery*! Although, personally, I don't think the miniseries did her justice."

Jackie replied with a knowing, humble grin. "You and me both."

The heavy front door swung open one last time as the last Christmas guest arrived. A cartload of luggage accompanied this one. Andy wondered who might arrive for a weekend getaway having packed for a full week. Or *even more*, as the mound showed.

Olivia shook her head in disgust as all three of them swiveled to get a look. There was someone even *more* spoiled and self-important than the Kenilworths themselves: Amelia Vanderkamp, chic and trim, with a figure only money and Ozempic could provide.

"Who's that?" Andy asked.

"Remember how I told you my brother broke off his engagement?" She gestured. "Meet Amelia Vanderkamp."

"As in *the* Vanderkamps?" Andy was impressed. "One of the richest families in the city?"

"The <u>country</u>, actually," Olivia replied, "Mother keeps a chart."

Amelia ambushed Liam, who had the misfortune of crossing the foyer at that moment. With an enthusiastic shout, she bellowed: "Liam!"

"Amelia?" He spun, equal parts shock and horror.

His reaction was not lost on the heiress, "I must admit, I was surprised your mother invited me.

"That makes two of us."

"But since I'm here... I was hoping we might talk?"

"I have nothing to say."

She gasped, not used to being dismissed. "You don't think you owe it to me? To us?"

"There is no us. I thought you understood. I thought *everyone* understood." Liam replied, motioning upstairs. It was no mystery to him who'd invited Amelia. Undoubtedly, it was the same matriarch who staged her own children's relationships as if strategically plotting place settings at a gala event.

"Oh good! We're all here!" The matriarch shouted. Margaret then descended the staircase with an arrogant aire of rehearsed choreography, designed to let everyone know who the belle of *this* Christmas ball really was.

"If you would, please join me in the dining room for a pre-game feast!"

"Amelia," she greeted her newest guest with a nod, as if watching her plotted puzzle pieces snap into place.

"Margaret," Amelia nodded in kind. Watching this mutual fawning, Liam shook his head. At least, until he caught Andy's eye. As they exchanged a smile, he forgot why he'd gotten annoyed in the first place, or that Amelia was even standing beside him.

That feeling wouldn't last.

The night's festivities were about to begin.

CHAPTER TWO

The family gathered around the long dining room table. Set with the finest holiday China, crystal stemware, and silver cutlery, the pristine specimen of antique furniture had been in the family longer than the lodge, and had witnessed many a tumultuous meal. Tonight would prove no exception. Not even Margaret's private chef, a *Michelin award winner*, as she was fond of reminding everyone at every opportunity, could whip up Christmas cheer from *this* family.

Raphael's spread of food, however, was *epic*. Canapés and hors d'oeuvres were adorned with edible gold leaf, while the pièce de résistance was a roasted pheasant stuffed with truffles and served with a cranberry reduction. Even the red and green cloth napkins were folded to resemble festive poinsettias. It was culinary artistry at its finest.

In the center of the table rose a magnificent silver candelabra, its ornate arms reaching upward like a frozen explosion of winter branches. Each of the candleholders held a pristine, ivory-colored taper candle, their flames flickering with a warm and inviting glow. Twisting tendrils of ivy, adorned with delicate white blossoms, cascaded down, creating an illusion of nature's embrace. Nestled within the ivy were clusters of glistening glass ornaments in shades of deep red, emerald green, and shimmering gold. They caught the light, casting reflections that danced across the room, adding a magical touch to the festive atmosphere.

Bridgette marched past the gathering family, with their soft murmurings of discontent, carrying a plate of homemade Christmas cookies. Indeed, such a treat could only be for one particular, special guest.

She placed the cookies down in front of Jackie Evenson, who gave her one of her warm, appreciative smiles. "Bless you," she said, nodding in gratitude for the delicious gift.

Leonora, upon tasting the evening's roasted pheasant, was far less gracious. Turning to Margaret, she remarked: "When you say *Michelin*, are you referring to the tires? Because this tastes like rubber."

Her husband, Olivia's uncle Gary, scoffed at her sister's attempts to astound her guests. "It's so cute how she's trying to impress us," he said with a snooty sneer. "I don't recall anyone complaining about the caviar from Zabars last year."

Jackie, eager to introduce some levity to the proceedings, turned to her friend and host. "Margaret," she offered with a smile. "Sounds like things at Kenilworth Enterprises have been going well?"

"Double last year's revenue," Margaret grinned. "In fact, I've been thinking about expanding."

"I wouldn't take any victory laps just yet," Gary shook his head, not about to let his sister win this round. "It's all market trends. Construction is up. Ergo, people need concrete. It won't last."

"That wouldn't affect your real estate market as well?" Margaret asked.

"People will <u>always</u> need housing," Gary remarked. "I'm actually headed back later to close on a new property tomorrow."

"Twenty units. Park view," Leonora announced, boasting of her husband's success.

Margaret launched another volley. "You came all this way just to hit up your sister for money?"

"And..." Gary countered, "to see all of you."

Amelia, who'd been born with a stick up her rear to match the silver spoon in her mouth, dressed down the stranger among them: Andy. "Candace," she said, using the name she despised. "Margaret tells me you're a waitress?"

Olivia jumped in to rescue her friend. "It's actually just Andy…"

"*Barista*," Andy defended herself. "Part time. Just until I finish paying off my student loans."

"She's a very talented writer," Olivia boasted on Andy's behalf. "She has a degree in creative writing from Berkeley."

Jackie, not about to let Andy succumb to the disdain of the one percent, offered: "My first job out of school was writing instruction manuals for DVD players."

"Well," Margaret sneered, "at least I know who to call if I need a latte."

"*Mother*." An embarrassed Liam exclaimed under his breath.

Eager to stay the focus of attention, Amelia stood, drawing all eyes to her. If she was not yet a Kenilworth by name, she was determined to act the part. "If I could have your attention? A toast! To exciting business ventures, present and future," she said, raising her glass and, shooting Liam a pointed glance, "the company of loved ones!"

The family toasted, much to Liam's chagrin. This was going exactly the way his mother had planned. Her desire to blend the Kenilworth and Vanderkamp bloodlines was no secret. Even Jackie, eager to undercut the tension with some humor, joined in the toast using two of her Christmas cookies instead of a drink.

Watching all of this from her seat, Andy no doubt felt grateful that, at least for the moment, she was spared the family's ire. She just didn't know how long that respite would last.

Unfortunately, it would not be long enough.

Game night was about to begin.

THE LARGE, GLEAMING blade of a knife plunged down with a firm ferocity! Its victim was a Christmas chocolate yule log, bleeding vanilla cream from the center as the blade sliced into its dark brown flesh.

"My famous Buche de Noel," Raphael announced, slicing his dessert for the guests.

"Yes please!" Olivia bounded over, plate in hand.

As the others gathered in the great room, waiting for their dessert, Olivia took her slice over to the drink table. There she found her brother, filling a red Christmas mug from a stainless-steel urn of hot cocoa. As Liam scooped tiny marshmallows into his cup from the smorgasbord of toppings, he nodded in Jackie's direction and grinned.

"Twenty bucks says she asks for cookies," he whispered.

"Is there anything you won't bet on?" Olivia sighed, fixing her own cocoa.

"Thirty?"

"You're on."

The siblings watched as Jackie approached Raphael. It looked like she was about to take a slice of cake, but then demurred.

"You wouldn't have any milk and cookies, would you?" she asked with a twinkle in her eye.

"Of course, mademoiselle," he smiled.

"Take your time. I'm still full of that *absolutely delightful* dinner," she gushed. Leonora shot her a disdainful look of disagreement.

"Merci," Raphael beamed.

Having witnessed the exchange, Liam just grinned at Olivia. The only thing he liked more than a good wager was the rush of victory. Unfortunately, his joy would be short-lived. Margaret approached her son, and, making yet another effort in her ongoing matchmaking pursuit, motioned to Amelia.

"You've barely said a word to her all night," Margaret said to Liam. "Do you have any idea what that girl is worth? Would it kill you to talk to her?"

"You're something else," he replied, shaking his head. He walked away, passing Andy, who sat self-consciously on the couch by the warm glow of the Christmas tree, trying to stay well outside the line of fire. Leonora, Amelia and Jackie were deep in conversation, debating the business practices of one Ebeneezer Scrooge.

"It's Christmas." Jackie noted. "It's supposed to be a time for giving."

"To whom?" Leonora snapped. "The man had no family."

"What about his long-time employee?" Olivia contributed as she sat down. "Who, might I add, had a disabled son!"

"In that case," Amelia scoffed. "Bob should have qualified for a government subsidy."

"In *Victorian England*?" Olivia asked.

Jackie leaned into Andy, rolling her eyes. "I'm not sure they got the point of the story."

"I'm not sure they even read it," Andy remarked with a grin. Jackie laughed. But then, Andy heard a noise.

"Anyone hear that?" She asked the room with concern.

Remembering the earlier incident in her room, she wasn't about to let this encounter go without investigation. She walked to the double glass doors overlooking the back of the lodge. She could make out bushes moving outside! Jackie, having heard the sound as well, soon joined her.

"I think there's someone out there!" Andy exclaimed. Jackie nodded.

The door burst open! Startled, Andy shrieked in fear as a man barged into the room! He wore a red jacket and red pants, with a bushy white beard and round belly, which shook when he laughed, like a bowl full of jelly.

"Ho ho ho," the right jolly old elf bellowed. Upon closer inspection, Andy realized it was Gary, stuffed into an elaborate Santa Claus costume. Over his shoulder he'd slung a large burlap sack overflowing with wrapped gifts. Each was long, thin, and rectangular.

"Merry Christmas!" Gary thundered in his best, bassy Kris Kringle impression.

"Every year, Santa brings the games for game night," Liam whispered to Andy. "The newest guest gets to choose one."

She realized he was referring to her. But she didn't feel ready for that responsibility. "It's okay. Someone else can do it."

"We couldn't *possibly* neglect a cherished, longstanding tradition," Liam grinned, not about to let it go.

Jackie encouraged Andy. "Go on. Make it a good one."

"Or better yet, *none at all*," grumbled the young Harper, with one of her trademark teen eye rolls, "Then we can just be done for the night."

Unable to dodge the responsibility, Andy just shrugged and chose a package. She tore through the Christmas wrapping paper, eager to get the moment over with.

Inside was a board game, just as she'd expected. It happened to be a game that she and Olivia had played incessantly as children: *Whodunit*, a social deduction game whose mechanics would be familiar to anyone who'd ever looked for Colonel Mustard in the library with the candlestick. How convenient, she thought, that she would choose the *one* game she and her best friend had spent hours playing as little girls?

"*Whodunit*!" Andy exclaimed to Olivia. "We used to play this at camp! Everyone picks a card, and the object of the game is to figure out which player goes with which identity..."

Olivia laughed. How could she forget? "You were so good at it too!"

Her curiosity piqued, Jackie extended her hand. "Mind if I look?"

Andy handed her the box. Jackie opened it to reveal a game board, its intricate design resembling a floor plan of a mansion not unlike the lodge. This "mansion" was divided into different rooms and different floors. Beneath the board was a stack of game cards, each of which was emblazoned with a unique identity. *The Thief, The Gambler*, and so forth.

"Put the silly board game away." Margaret interrupted, making her way to the front of the room. "I have something more... *interesting* in mind."

All eyes watched with bated breath, curious about what, in Margaret's eyes, could be interesting.

"This year," Margaret announced, "we're going to play a *new* game. I call it *Windfall*.

I won't lie. Financially, I have had a marvelous year. Revenue is way up and my dividends have paid well. So, in the spirit of giving, I've decided that I'm going to *share* my good fortune... with *one of you*."

"Oh, come now," Gary said with a huff, "you don't expect us to believe that *you,* Margaret Kenilworth, are going to share your money with us."

"First of all, I said *one* of you." Margaret snapped at her brother. "Second of all, I said nothing about money."

Everyone exchanged glances, their interest building.

"The object of the game is simple." Margaret continued. "You're going to pitch why *you* and you *alone* deserve the prize. And the winner..."

She reached down and pulled out a familiar, large jewelry box. Opening it, she revealed the evening's prize.

"...gets *my Christmas Diamond*."

Everyone's eyes widened as she lifted the necklace. It was huge. Priceless. *Flawless.* Glistening with green and red from the exquisite rubies and emeralds.

"One of you *vultures* will get this diamond tonight," she said with a conceited grin, "And, since my son is so *fond of tradition...*"

She turned to Andy. "*...our guest* will choose who!"

Feeling the attention turn in her direction, Andy couldn't deflect the proverbial hot potato fast enough. "Oh no, no... I couldn't possibly..."

"It's okay," Liam sought to calm her nerves. "It's only a game."

"Is it, now?" Margaret smirked with a spiteful smile. Turning back to Andy, she continued. "No pressure, dear. All you must do is decide... *who* gets the Christmas Diamond."

Andy looked at the sparkling necklace. And then her eyes fell upon each of the family members, who salivated at the sight of the gem. She swallowed hard as Jackie watched on with a smile... and a cookie. And then, offering both a smile and observation, the author spoke.

"Let the games begin."

CHAPTER TWO

If Margaret Kenilworth wanted attention, then she had it. Everyone in the room watched her. The Christmas Diamond could be theirs? That was better than *any* gift they could have ever dreamed of. The only question now was, who would be the lucky winner, and which poor sucker would walk away with only lumps of coal in their stocking?

Each of them sized up the competition, knowing that their pitch, their *one chance* to win Margaret's game of so-called "Windfall," had better be special. Who most deserved the diamond? Not to mention, which was the better strategy: business acuity or the willingness to grovel at the feet of their host, who grew giddy at the prospect of pitting the vultures against one another?

"So please," Margaret said, gazing over the contenders, "each of you take a moment and consider your pitch carefully."

"I don't need a moment," Gary spoke first, launching into his pitch. "The answer is obvious. Everyone knows precious metals and gems are the most stable investments on the market right now. I'm the only person in this room who can *guarantee* to triple its value. Minus a *small percentage* for myself, of course."

Margaret nodded with approval, impressed with the idea that her selfless gesture would somehow result in a net gain for herself. "Anyone else care to make me an offer?"

Her daughter, Olivia, spoke next. "What about Bridgette?"

Gary was puzzled at his niece's suggestion. "The *maid*?"

"Butler." Bridgette corrected him.

"Let's be honest," Olivia continued with her generous pitch. "Does anyone else here really need it?"

"Candace does," Amelia offered, never missing an opportunity to knock someone down a peg.

"I'm good, thanks," Andy demurred.

"Oh sweetie," Amelia purred. "I've seen your car. You are not *good*."

Gary wasn't about to give up. "No offense to Bridgette or Andy, but in terms of *potential return...*"

"Maybe she just wants someone to *have* the Diamond." Liam interrupted.

"You just want it for yourself." Gary huffed to his nephew.

Liam grinned. Gary, of course, was right. "Well in all fairness, *everyone* knows *I* love her the most!" Then, with a kiss: "Right, mother?"

"It *would* help me launch my fashion line." Olivia noted. Andy was relieved someone had found a positive use for the money.

"Oh? Business not exactly booming?" Leonora sneered.

"Excuse me if we're not all buying up real estate," Olivia snapped.

"If you're going to give it to one of the *kids*," Harper finally seemed to pay attention. "At least give it to the one still in school. I mean, do you even *have* designs?"

"Jackie?" Margaret turned to her friend who'd remained quiet. "How about you? Care to make a pitch?"

"I'm perfectly comfortable, thank you." Jackie turned her attention back to her cookie.

"Are you sure?" Margaret never could just let something go. "Could buy you a bigger house."

"I'm a divorcee with no children living in a five-bedroom house," Jackie pointed out. "I have more than enough space."

"Perhaps Raphael could use it to buy himself another award!" Leonora sneered at her favorite Michelin-winning target.

"I *earned* that award!" The chef shouted back in his French accent.

"My pallet begs to differ."

"Your pallet would prefer fast food!" He shook his head and stomped out, propelled by his self-important Gallic temper.

"Andy." Margaret had heard enough. "Have you made your decision?"

"I appreciate you putting your trust in me," Andy replied, "but honestly... I wouldn't even know where to begin."

At that moment Margaret sneered with such derision that Andy realized she'd been the butt of one of her host's cruel and abusive jokes. "Oh, you silly girl," she snickered. "I would *never* put my trust in *you*. Did anyone really think I'd let *her* decide what to do with *my* diamond? I've made my decision! And I've decided the diamond is going to..."

She paused, relishing the feeling of holding the room in her palm. Like the figurines she stored in the guest room, Andy knew Margaret saw the world, and, by extension, everyone in it, as her plaything.

"...*none of you*." Margaret announced, snapping the box shut.

The room erupted in anger. The family members shouted at one another in disappointed protest.

"That's just cruel, mother." Olivia shook her head.

Liam was disgusted. "Low, even for you."

"Bridgette," Margaret said, looking down her nose at her butler. "Perhaps *these children* would like more hot cocoa?"

The butler nodded, as if she had no choice but to humor her employer's casual cruelty. "Yes ma'am."

"My sister just *loves* lording over the rest of us, doesn't she?" Gary stood up in disgust. He wasn't about to let Margaret placate him with refreshment.

"Could she be any nastier?" Leonora whispered to her husband.

But then, as if punctuating the dramatic outburst, Bridgette tripped, spilling her tray of hot cocoa onto Leonora!

"My dress!" Leonora exclaimed, regarding the large brown stain on the front of her expensive outfit. "Do you have any idea how much this costs?"

"It was an accident," Liam interjected.

"My family has fired maids for less!" Amelia snapped with condensation.

"Mrs. Kenilworth, if you'd just..." Bridgette tried to defend herself.

"Amelia's right." Margaret snapped. "*You're fired.*"

Bridgette couldn't believe her ears. Years of working for this wretched woman, catering to her ever-spoiled whim, and this is what it came down to? The casualness with which someone disregarded her years of loyalty was more hurtful than any insult. She fled the room, tears welling in her eyes, much to Andy's horror and disgust. Surely Bridgette deserved better!

"It's Christmas!" Andy exclaimed.

But Margaret just crossed her arms. "Then, in the spirit of the season, let me give you some advice. *Never forget your place.*" With that, the woman turned to her niece, Harper. While Andy didn't know why, the message had been intended for her as well.

Whatever the reason, it drove the young woman from the room.

HARPER FINALLY FOUND a quiet place in the kitchen to gather her thoughts. It was far from her family, far from the parents who hovered over her, and far from the caustic, disapproving aunt. That's when the young girl spotted a tray of drinks sitting on the counter.

Harper picked up a glass. She sniffed its contents. It was inviting. *Maybe this one time*, she thought. *Maybe just a sip.*

"Excuse me!" Her mother Leonora shouted from across the room.

"Please," Harper scoffed. "As if I haven't had a hundred of these things."

"Since *when?*" Her mother demanded.

"Wow, mom," Harper rolled her eyes. "You really *are* oblivious."

With her quiet respite interrupted, Harper tried to leave. Leonora stopped her. "Not until we talk."

"I wouldn't want to take you away from my aunt's money."

"Is that what you think?"

"You don't even like these people!"

"We don't have to. They're family."

"Finally," Harper laughed. "The first honest thing you've said all day."

And with that, the young girl stormed away, her mother hovering close behind as usual.

BACK IN THE GREAT ROOM, the party had dissolved into a cacophony of tense barking. Liam pulled Andy aside. "Moment of truth. On a scale of one to ten, ten being an absolute train wreck..."

"Ten," Andy laughed. "Definitely ten."

"You always had the cutest laugh," Liam confided in her, remembering their past. "Do you remember one summer we made those dreamcatchers at camp...?"

Andy nodded. "And you got your arm all tangled? You were in so much pain!"

"You laughed *so hard*," Liam grinned, picturing it as if it were just that morning, "your Mountain Dew spurted from your nose!"

"You remember that?"

"I'm pretty sure my sister has Polaroids of that too, somewhere." Liam smiled, making Andy laugh again. And then, his smile faded into something else, something more emotional than either of them would have expected. "The one and only *Candy Kayne*. I still can't believe you're here."

Andy looked up, as they both noticed that they were standing beneath under a sprig of mistletoe.

"And not just *here*," Liam noticed the mistletoe as well. "But also, under, you know..."

"We couldn't *possibly* neglect a cherished, longstanding tradition." Andy smiled, using Liam's own words against him.

Their lips grew close. Their hearts grew even closer. At least, until Amelia shoved them both aside. Storming out in a dramatic, and purposeful, display of temper. The damage, however, was done. The moment Andy and Liam shared, deep as it was, had passed.

"You know, we should probably..." Liam began, deflecting. He then turned to the empty hot chocolate urn. "Oh! I should, you know, make more cocoa..."

Andy sensed an opportunity to get away from the tense room. "Oh no, no, *I* could..."

"Yeah, Liam," Gary grinned. "How about we have *the professional* make some coffee? I, for one, would love an espresso."

Andy smiled and inspired by Gary's suggestion, rude as it may have been, turned to Liam. "Tell me. Have you ever had a spiced gingerbread latte?"

"Can't say I've had the pleasure."

"Then today is your lucky day," Andy grinned, leaving with the empty urn.

Andy carried the urn through the foyer just in time to catch the end of Leonora and Harper's argument. It reminded her of Margaret and Olivia, and she realized that *both* sides of the family dripped with dysfunction. In fact, the image was still playing over and over in Andy's mind when she approached the espresso machine in the kitchen. The machine was a modern marvel of technology, and far more complicated than a home kitchen should require.

If only they'd had a machine like that in the coffee shop, she thought to herself, as she packed the ingredients she needed for Liam's spiced gingerbread latte. While here, it would go unused now that someone had fired the butler. Would Margaret's French

Michelin-award-winning chef be willing to reduce himself to resident coffee maker? Unlikely.

For a moment, she thought about assuming the responsibility herself. It would keep her close to Liam. But she dismissed the notion. They weren't children anymore. They were adults. They no longer had time to indulge themselves in a cutesy summer camp crush.

But at least for now, Liam would get his Christmas latte. She pressed the Brew button.

And that was when the entire lodge went dark.

IMMERSED IN DARKNESS, the family, still gathered in the great room, panicked. The lodge, now without power, was as quiet as a tomb. The Christmas lights now hung dark in the shadows.

Leonora noticed Olivia growing uncomfortable. "Oh, grow up."

"Leave the poor girl alone," Jackie spoke up in her defense. "Being afraid of the dark is nothing to be ashamed of." Then, leaning over, she took Olivia's hand and whispered, "Me too."

"My sister can say whatever she wants about me," Gary groaned. "At least *I* remember the pay the power bill every month."

"Relax, Uncle Gary," Liam said. "It's just a fuse."

"Fine. Just stay right there." Gary contributed, eager to project confidence and control. "I'll be right back."

"Where are you going?" his wife asked.

"To take this thing off," he showed the Santa suit, "and find the circuit breaker."

"I'll help," Liam said, his mind trying to remember all those times his computers, with their fantasy football and online poker, had played havoc with the old lodge's wiring, and where the breaker panel had been located.

Someone less familiar with the lodge, however, stood in the kitchen. Uncertain what to do next, Andy thought about trying to feel her way through the darkness, hoping she might retrace her steps back to the great room. She knew Olivia and Liam would be there, and that would be preferable to being alone. After all, the only thing worse than being all alone in a large, creepy house was being all alone in a large, creepy house *in the dead of night*.

But then, in that very darkness, something outside the window caught Andy's attention. A car parked out front. Sitting ominously with its headlights off, a cloud of exhaust encased the vehicle. It was impossible to tell if there was anyone in the vehicle or if it were idling empty.

However, before Andy could reach a decision on what to do next... the lights came back on! Once again, she could see her surroundings, and she felt a certain protection. At least, she did until what followed next.

An ear-splitting SHRIEK!

It was Margaret. Everyone in the lodge knew instantly. After all, she never restrained herself from raising her voice at the slightest provocation: real or imagined. Everyone had heard that shrill tone before at least once, and at an uncomfortable volume.

Everyone went running to see what the matter was.

Liam raced down the stairs to find his mother emerging from her home office, shaken. This was the unusual part. Not the outburst. Not the piercing decibel level. It was her *fear* that caught him off guard. Neither he nor his sister could recall a single time that Margaret had been afraid of anything. Whenever Margaret would pay a visit to the office, it was *her own employees* who cowered in trepidation. But sure enough, on this fateful evening, Liam found his mother in a state of fright, and it was discomforting. Whatever took place just moments earlier must have been *undeniably* momentous.

"Where did they go?" Margaret cried out upon seeing her son.

"Where'd who go?" he replied, still puzzled.

And then, as if she could barely bring herself to say the words, "My diamond. Someone stole the Christmas Diamond!"

Liam heard a noise coming down the hall. It was Andy, returning from the kitchen to see what had happened. Could she have witnessed something?

"Andy, did you see anyone?" he asked, knowing full well that, until moments ago, she too was stranded in darkness.

"Just the car outside," she replied.

But that was all Liam needed to hear.

By the time Liam burst through the front door to confront the car, it was gone. Andy, reliable to a fault, and not known to be a fabulist, was confused.

"I'm telling you!" she exclaimed. "It was *right there*!"

"So, they got away." Liam replied, disappointed.

Gary emerged from behind them, still half-dressed in his Santa suit. "What's going on? What's all the ruckus?"

"Looks like *someone* got the Diamond after all." Liam sighed.

"The Christmas Diamond is missing?" Gary wanted to make sure he'd heard right. After all, he knew his sister had always guarded the gaudy gem with her life.

By this time, a small cluster of guests gathered in the doorway. Jackie, for one, seemed eager for details. Birdie Pickett herself could not have wished for a more appropriate way to spend a holiday party.

"Forget game night." Jackie turned to Andy. "Looks like we've got ourselves a genuine mystery!"

CHAPTER THREE

Margaret watched as the frantic whirlwind of searching tore apart her great room. Furniture was upended, rugs pulled, and pillows flipped. By the time Liam, Olivia, Gary and Leonora finished, the space looked like it was eligible for disaster relief.

It seemed the only thing the maelstrom did *not* turn up...

...was the Christmas Diamond.

"It has to be here somewhere!" Leonora exclaimed in frustration.

"Hope so!" Gary responded, checking the Rolex he couldn't afford. "I have to leave soon!"

"No one's going *anywhere*," Margaret declared. "Not until we find my diamond! I'm calling Billings."

Andy turned to Liam and whispered, "Who's Billings?"

"A detective with the Tahoe Police Department," he said with concern.

"You'd be surprised how much influence money can buy you," Olivia noted.

Gary, meanwhile, had heard enough of his sister's ranting. "For crying out loud, you probably just forgot where you put it!"

"No," she snapped. "I'd already put it in the safe, which means someone *took* it! And... since the rest of the staff had already left, my money is on *one of you*."

She scanned their faces. Each of them avoided direct eye contact. Was it guilt? Or was it that they didn't like her? And who could blame them? It was behavior like this that earned her a toxic reputation.

"Until we figure out *who*," she continued, "*everyone* is staying put."

Gary grumbles under his breath. He was going to miss his flight, thanks to his sister and her crackpot delusions of persecution.

That's when the lodge's main gate swung shut. So heavy and so massive, the sound thundered throughout the lodge. If anyone had a desire to leave the property that evening, they'd stand a better chance penetrating Fort Knox.

Returning to the study, Jackie examined the safe while, standing behind her, the family whispered their not-so-secret suspicions. Surely it couldn't have been a Kenilworth. *Not one of the privileged.*

"Maybe it was that horrid chef," mused Leonora, never missing an opportunity to skewer her favored target du jour. "Or that clumsy maid."

"Butler," Andy defended Bridgette. The poor woman had already lost her job tonight, she didn't need to lose her reputation as well.

"Bridgette already *had* the Diamond," Olivia pointed out. "If she wanted it, she could have kept it."

With no theories of her own, Andy turned to the one person among them who might stand a chance at solving the mystery. After all, mysteries were Jackie's bread and butter.

"What do you think?" Andy whispered.

"Shhh," Jackie hushed her, content to eavesdrop for the time being. "The first rule of crime solving is *observation*."

"What about Andy?" Amelia asked. It did not surprise Andy to become a target of suspicion. After all, she wasn't *one of them*.

"Amelia..." Liam uttered under his breath.

"No, no." Olivia spoke up, insulted by the attack on her friend. "I want to hear this. Go on."

"Being a woman of limited means," Amelia replied. "I'm guessing she's up to her eyeballs in student debt."

"So that makes her a criminal?" Liam raised an eyebrow to his ex-girlfriend's reasoning.

"Frankly, if anyone's acting suspicious around here, it's *you*, Uncle Gary." Olivia pointed a finger.

"What do you mean?" Gary stammered.

"Why the sudden hurry to leave?" she demanded.

"I told you; I have to close a deal."

"Right," replied an incredulous Olivia. "Tell us how successful your business is again?"

"Why?" he huffed.

"Because *truly* successful people don't have to keep reminding people how successful they are!"

"Clearly you've never been to New York," Leonora scoffed.

But Olivia was just warming up. "And *you*!" She turned to Harper. "Where were you?"

"She was talking to me!" Leonora jumped in.

"Then I went outside to take a phone call," Harper replied.

Margaret's eyes narrowed with suspicion. "How? I took your phone."

"My *other* phone," Harper admitted, only to get one of her mother's exasperated looks. "I'm an influencer. My phone is my life!"

"Keep saying that," Liam snickered. "Maybe it'll actually come true."

And with that, Harper stormed out. Gary, all too familiar with his daughter's teenaged temper, cried after her. "Sweetkins?"

But it was too late. "Sweetkins" was already gone. The only thing her father could do was follow her. And follow her he did, out into the hallway. Soon the whole family poured out, watching the squabble. Sometimes, reality was *more* entertaining than reality television.

"Sweetkins!" Gary shouted after her a second time. While his voice echoed throughout the empty lodge, it did little to deter the teen.

Frustrated, Gary spun around to confront Liam. "Before you go pointing fingers at my little girl, I'd look a little closer to home!"

"Why would *I* steal *my mother's* Christmas Diamond?" Liam rolled his eyes.

"I dunno." Gary shrugged. "Why wouldn't you know where the circuit breakers were in your own house?"

"Because it's not *my* house. It's my mother's *winter* home," he protested.

"You mean it was *her husband's.*" Gary never missed an opportunity for sibling rivalry. "Still, you *have* spent more time here than anyone else in this room. You and *your sister.*"

"Don't go dragging *me* into this, Uncle Gary!" Olivia protested.

"Yes. What *about* Olivia?" Leonora piled on with her husband.

"What *about* me?" Olivia demanded.

"A million-dollar diamond is better than collecting unemployment," Leonora sneered.

"Who said anything about being unemployed?" asked Olivia.

Gary jumped in. "You're the one who said you needed the money for your work."

"Because I wanted to start my own company!" Olivia announced. "If you *must* know, the company I work for just finished designing a new sneaker line for a pro athlete, and I had to sign an NDA. So, you'll forgive me if I don't put myself in legal trouble just to impress you."

Andy had an idea and tried to interject. "Excuse me..."

Margaret turned, arms crossed, and looked down on her daughter's friend with disdain. "Oh good. Candace is ready to confess."

"*Actually,*" Andy corrected her. "I was going to suggest that we search our rooms."

"*Our* rooms?" Gary huffed.

"Andy's right," Jackie spoke up. "It's likely our thief would either have the diamond *on* them... or they've *stashed* it."

"This is ridiculous," Gary scoffed.

"The sooner we find it, the sooner we can all leave," Andy pointed out.

"Although... she has a point." Gary nodded, thinking about the plane ticket burning a hole in his pocket and the fact that he needed to be back in the city by Christmas.

Amelia, however, was less convinced. "And if I say I don't want Candace going through my things?"

"Then I'd say you're *hiding something*," Andy said.

Margaret turned to her friend, the mystery professional. "Jackie, you're an impartial party. Would you mind leading the search?"

"Not at all," Jackie replied before turning to Andy. "However, I would like *her* to come along."

Andy tried to hide her excitement behind a shield of humility. After all, her favorite author just requested a collaboration. "Jackie, you don't have to..."

"Pish posh." Jackie wouldn't let up. "As of this moment, you are my assistant. And the game is afoot, my dear Watson!"

IF THERE WAS ANYTHING the Kenilworth family valued more than money, it was privacy. Now, thanks to Margaret, their rooms, their luggage, and their possessions, were all about to be studied by the two true outsiders among them. Whether it was Harper's French dictionaries, Gary's "Real Estate for Dummies" books, or the naughty negligee that Amelia packed hoping to ensnare Liam... Jackie and Andy had access to all of it. And who would have thought that Olivia, well into her 20s, would have such an extensive collection of stuffed animals. It seemed the adage was true. *Once a princess, always a princess.*

By the time they'd gotten to Leonore's medicine bag, which contained enough sleeping pills to tranquilize a medium-sized barnyard animal, they'd just about given up. While they'd observed enough material to keep the family gossip mill churning for the next decade, there wasn't a missing Christmas gem to be found.

But, leaving the spartan room of Liam behind, Andy heard a noise coming from down the hall. There was nothing back there except the attic door, so it made little sense for there to be a sound. Yet, *there it was*. A creepy sound, coming from the creepy darkness, in a creepy old house. For a moment, Andy wondered whose novel she was living in: Jackie Evenson or Stephen King.

There was only one way to be sure.

She turned on her phone's flashlight and stepped into the dark attic.

If the bedrooms had been a window into the vapid lives of the rich and infamous, then the attic was a museum immortalizing the vanity of one of the wealthiest families on the West Coast. Many articles were written about the rise and domination of Kenilworth Enterprises. Their concrete was used in some of the best-known buildings in the 20th century. One could make a case that the foundation of San Francisco itself was built on the family's achievements.

Andy searched with curiosity. There was so much to investigate in the murky labyrinth of heirlooms and treasures. Wedding dresses that all but the moths had forgotten. Priceless books rendered worthless by poor storage and exposure. And through it all, Andy could not shake the feeling that she wasn't alone.

Thump-thump.

Her heart pounded in her chest as she approached the dark, unlit corner of the room.

Thump-thump.

Thump-thump.

Something lurched forward! Shoving Andy's tiny frame to the ground! It then raced to get away! Andy, startled and terrified, ignored the instinct to run and hide. Instead, she reached to grab at it. *Perhaps this was the thief! Biding their time until they had the perfect opportunity to escape!*

However, clutching the shadowy intruder, Andy heard a familiar British accent.

"You're hurting me!" The voice cried out.

Andy pulled this stranger into the light and realized; it was no stranger at all.

It was Bridgette. The butler.

LESS THAN A HALF HOUR later, the butler sat on the couch in the great room, by the light of that same majestic Christmas tree, confronted by a tribunal composed of Margaret, Jackie, and Andy. The two more sympathetic among them watched as the third glowered with indigent rage. Even in silence, Margaret had an intimidating way about her. And now, Bridgette, whose resilient family had braved the encephalitis pandemic, the 1956 London smog, *and* the deadly 1976 British heat wave, was terrified of *this woman*.

"I swear," Bridgette said, her voice breaking, "I only came back for a few things." Turning to Margaret, she then challenged her: "You've always been kind to me. Why would I hurt you?"

Jackie turned to Andy and whispered, "Margaret is many things. Kind is not one of them."

"I didn't even come back inside until <u>after</u> the power went out," Bridgette continued. "I thought it might be a chance to grab a few things I'd forgotten."

Andy remembered what she saw earlier in the evening, and a puzzle piece clicked into place. "You ordered a ride, didn't you? That explains the car I saw!"

Jackie nodded. Andy had solved part of the mystery on her own.

"Well," Margaret addressed her onetime employee. "I suppose since you're back here, you might as well help."

"I'm no longer fired?" The butler asked, her voice rising with hope.

"Consider it... *probation*," Margaret said. It seemed even her positive comments came with caveats or conditions.

But then, the interrogation was interrupted by another unexpected development. Amelia entered the room, her arms crossed. She had news to share and, from the look in her eyes, Andy suspected it wouldn't be good.

"I found something you're all going to want to see." Amelia announced.

"In whose room?" Margaret demanded.

And that was when Amelia's finger lowered, pointing at one specific individual. Andy. "Hers."

It seemed Margaret couldn't get to Andy's room fast enough. Now, thanks to Amelia's own investigation, which focused on a single suspect, she had the ammunition she needed to accuse the one person she felt didn't belong. The guest whose very presence was forced upon her.

Racing into Andy's room, Margaret found her luggage sitting on the bed. The zipper on the rolling bag had already been undone, by Amelia herself. Margaret tore through its contents like a hungry vulture feasting on its dead dinner. From the second the diamond disappeared, Andy wondered exactly *when* the blame would point her way.

When that moment arrived, it did not disappoint.

It wasn't *evidence* that Margaret found, buried deep beneath pairs of Target-brand jeans and sweaters that were purchased at Old Navy...

...it was the Christmas Diamond itself.

CHAPTER FOUR

Moments later, the Christmas Diamond Inquisition had reassembled. Only this time, the venue was Andy's room. And the suspect was now Andy herself. Once again, the young woman was the center of attention.

And it was all Amelia's fault, the would-be romantic rival who was now rifling through the rest of Andy's luggage.

"Do you really have to...?" Andy started. But Amelia just shot her a sharp glance that stopped the thought cold.

Margaret, meanwhile, sized Andy up with cruel, judgmental eyes. The Christmas Diamond swung on its chain, dangling from her tight grip. It was unlikely she'd ever let it out of her sight again. Andy could see traits of one of her favorite literary characters within the crone's covetous eyes. A character who had also valued a piece of jewelry over everything *and everyone* else. She could almost hear Margaret utter those infamous words. *My precioussss.*

Instead, what she *did* utter were plain, disdainful accusations. "I knew from the moment I laid eyes on her...!"

"You can always tell a person based on their family," Amelia chimed in, proverbial poison dripping from the silver spoon planted in her mouth.

Jackie whispered, offering Andy one of her Christmas cookies in a paper bag. "You look like you need one of these."

"Thanks, but I'm not hungry."

Jackie shrugged and took one for herself. The sweetness of the dough and the chocolate chip provided a needed respite from the uncomfortable cynicism filling the room.

"Did no one else think it was a coincidence," Andy spoke up in her own defense, casting a bitter glance at Amelia, "that *she*, of all people, just found it in *my* suitcase?"

"Me of all people?" Amelia huffed. "Why, Candace? Because you're trying to hook up with my fiancée?"

"*Ex*-fiancée," Andy retorted.

"You <u>do</u> like him!" Amelia exclaimed.

"I... I didn't say that." Andy demurred, breaking eye contact.

Jackie leaned in to her protégé with another whisper. "Curious."

"What is?" Andy replied.

"You broke eye contact when said that. But <u>not</u> when you said you didn't steal the necklace."

"I don't suppose nervous habits are admissible in court?" Andy asked.

"I'm afraid not," Jackie replied.

"Then I think I'll have one after all." Andy said, reaching into Jackie's cookie bag.

That's when Amelia, still going through Andy's clothes, patted the pocket. She'd found something. Her gaze fell upon Andy, relishing her uncomfortable guilt.

"What's *this*?" Amelia asked as she pulled out the Hummel figurine that Andy had pocketed earlier. The Little Drummer Boy now sat in her palm, clutched tight by her manicured nails.

"Give me that!" Margaret gasped, reaching for the tiny percussionist. "I brought this back from Rödental myself thirty years ago! "

Andy's heart pounded. She remembering the series of events that had led to her to pocket the small figurine. As well as the encounter with Detective Billings that caused it to remain there.

"I wasn't going to take it," Andy started. "I just…"

"You just… *what*?" Margaret demanded.

"I forgot it was in my pocket!" Andy blurted.

But Margaret had heard enough. First her Christmas Diamond, then one of her prized figurines? She shook her head with disdain and then, did the only thing she felt she could do. She pulled out her phone and dialed the Lake Tahoe police department.

"Captain Billings please," she said to the voice on the other end. "Margaret Kenilworth, it's urgent."

"Mrs. Kenilworth…" Andy tried to interject.

But Margaret raised her hand to silence her, continuing into the phone: "I realize it's late, but when *will* you expect him…? Yes, he'll know who I am. Thank you."

She hung up. All the while, Andy continued trying to defend herself.

"I told you," she explained. "It was an accident!"

Margaret didn't believe her for one second. "You *honestly* expect me to believe you just *accidentally* pocketed a collectible worth five thousand dollars?"

"Who knows what *else* she might be capable of!" Amelia exclaimed.

Jackie had a much more thoughtful response, slipping into her comfortable detective role. "Your security cameras… I assume they're recording?"

"You'd have to ask Liam in the morning," Margaret said. "He set them up."

"Very well," Jackie said, turning to Andy. "This is over."

Margaret stood. "We're not finished."

"This may be your winter lodge, Margaret." Jackie said, asserting herself to her friend for the first time since she'd arrived. "But the girl is *still* innocent until proven guilty."

"Fine." Margaret headed for the door. "I'll prove her guilty."

Margaret and Amelia left. Andy doubt she'd be able to sleep knowing that her housemates were suspicious of her.

She stayed awake all night.

LIAM REMEMBERED THE day Margaret demanded they install a security system. The neighbor's house, at least a half mile away, had been burgled while its residents were vacationing in Marseilles. While the only intruder their cameras caught was a hungry black bear, Margaret was convinced she'd be next. After all, what enterprising young punk wouldn't want to get a hold of a collection of imported Hummels? So, at his mother's insistence, Liam installed a security system to rival the Federal Reserve.

But on this crisp winter morning, Margaret hoped that her security system had caught a thief in the act. More specifically, a *certain houseguest*. After all, it was unlikely that her diamond had been stolen by a 600-pound bear.

Sitting behind Margaret's desk in the study, mere feet away from the very safe where the theft occurred, Liam sat at his mother's charmingly vintage Dimension XPS computer with Jackie and Andy hovering over his shoulder. His sister Olivia paced behind them, torn between loyalties to her mother and the best friend who now pleaded for her understanding.

"Olivia, I swear," Andy said. "I took nothing from your mother!"

On the CRT monitor, everyone watched footage of the hallway that Liam had brought up from the previous night. They could see Margaret heading into the study, with no sign of anyone else. If they'd hoped that the camera caught a suspect, they would be disappointed.

The video then showed the moment that the lights went out. They saw Margaret burst back out in a panic. On screen, Liam rushed to help from the stairs, while Andy came from the kitchen.

"You see?" Andy exclaimed, pointing at the screen and feeling vindicated. "I was in the kitchen!"

"What about those blind spots?" Jackie asked, pointing to portions of the hallway that were obscured by the camera. "Is there another angle?"

"That's it for the hallway," Liam said, disappointed.

"But you would have seen me cross!" Andy pointed out. "There's no way I did it."

Olivia, however, knew otherwise. "Unless you took the other way out."

Puzzled, Jackie and Andy both turned to her in near unison. *There was another way out?*

But there was indeed. Olivia took them into the kitchen to demonstrate. There, at the very back of the gigantic space, behind an enormous door, was a very tiny elevator.

Jackie reached out and gave a tug on the copper-colored grill gate. "Where does this go?"

"The basement." Olivia replied, arms crossed.

"I didn't even know that was there!" Andy exclaimed upon seeing the old elevator for the first time.

"Maybe Liam told you." Olivia shrugged.

"But he didn't!" Andy replied.

"Or Bridgette," her friend continued. At this moment, she felt more like her mother than the former roommate. "You two seemed chummy."

"You have to admit, Andy," Jackie said, "It looks bad."

Andy sighed with frustration. Indeed, the elevator presented a way to have left the kitchen unseen. Andy's alibi was gone.

"Let's assume for a minute I did take the diamond." Andy said, turning to Jackie. "What do *you* think happened?"

Jackie paced. Her mind spun as a hypothesis formed. She grabbed a cookie out of her bag and took a nibble. This was her process. Somehow the combination of egg, sugar and flower caused the little grey cells of her brain to form solutions.

"Let's start with when you left the room," Jackie said. "Supposedly to make coffee."

"*Supposedly*?" Andy huffed.

"What if you used the secret elevator, went into the basement," Jackie suggested, "and turned off the power."

Jackie continued, "Then, with everyone assuming you were still in the kitchen, you went to the study and, with Margaret's back turned, took the diamond!"

While plausible, Andy found the image of herself sneaking around the house in a hidden elevator, committing grand larceny right under her host's nose, seemed ludicrous.

"Then what did she do?" Olivia asked.

"She went to the kitchen and waited for Gary to turn the power back on." Jackie finished. "You had the opportunity, the motive, and let us not forget, they found the item in *your* possession. That is all Margaret needs to give Detective Billings."

"They found it in *my bag*," Andy corrected her in self-defense. "I'd call that a pretty big difference."

"I'd call it *probable cause*." Jackie replied.

"Why would someone *put* it in your things?" Olivia pressed.

"Either the thief panicked when they found out we were searching the rooms," Andy said, "or... they're *deliberately setting me up*!"

"Who would do that?" Olivia demanded.

Andy's mind ran through the list of suspects. "Amelia. Or Margaret."

Seeing she wasn't quite convincing Jackie, Andy went for broke. "Tell you what. I'll make you a bet."

"Now you sound like Liam," Olivia shook her head.

"If I can poke *three* holes in your theory," Andy said to Jackie, throwing down the proverbial gauntlet. "You have to accept the possibility that someone is setting me up."

"And if you don't?" Jackie said.

"I'll drive to the police station myself." Andy shrugged.

Jackie imagined how their host might respond. "I doubt Margaret would give you the same chance."

"That's why I'm asking *you*," Andy said, knowing Jackie was right. "So how about it? Do you accept?"

All eyes fell to Jackie. Suspicions aside, she liked the cut of this audacious young woman's jib. "But humor me. Just how do you plan to pull off this minor miracle?"

Andy crossed her arms. "What would you say to a good, old-fashioned interrogation?"

Jackie grinned, channeling the very detective character that made her famous. More and more, this mystery was resembling one of her own creations. "I'd say... good idea. There's just one thing I require first."

THERE ARE SEVERAL TOOLS at an interrogator's disposal to elicit the truth from a suspect. Deceit is the most common; making the subject believe that their co-conspirators are ready to flip on them, thus inspiring them to flip first. Asking leading and loaded questions can also be a reliable technique, such as "how long did you wait after the homeowner left before breaking in?" Some prefer to mirror the suspects to establish rapport and empathy. Then there's the so-called Reid Technique, developed by John E. Reid in the 1950s, which was also known as "Good Cop, Bad Cop."

But Jackie was a big believer in using food. She knew nothing would gain a suspect's trust faster than a full stomach.

Here, the weapon of choice... would be cookies. These, however, would not be any ordinary cookies. Andy had something *very special* in mind for the occasion: her mother's secret cookie recipe.

Andy dug through the pantry and found a suitable holiday themed apron, adorned with colorful gingerbread men. She then gathered the ingredients: flour, sugar, brown sugar, baking soda, salt, butter, eggs, vanilla extract, and, of course, a generous helping of semisweet chocolate chips.

As she measured out the ingredients, the kitchen filled with a comforting aroma of vanilla and butter. Andy took her time, savoring each moment, as she knew that creating something magical took patience and love.

She began by whisking the softened butter and sugars until they formed a fluffy, pale mixture. Next, she added the eggs one at a time, mixing them into the butter and sugar with gentle strokes.

In a separate bowl, Andy combined the flour, baking soda, salt, and her mother's secret ingredients, with the exact contents and ratio hidden from view. The result was a fine, powdery mixture. The scent of the dough was heavenly, promising delights to come.

Finally, it was time for the most important ingredient: the semisweet chocolate chips. Andy folded them into the dough, watching as they disappeared into its depths. She could hardly resist sneaking a taste of the dough, which was a perfect blend of sweet and savory. Scoop in hand, Andy portioned the dough onto a baking sheet lined with parchment paper. She spaced them evenly, knowing that each cookie needed room to spread and become the perfect combination. Crispy on the edges but soft in the center.

Andy preheated the oven and slid the cookie-laden sheet inside. She set the timer and waited, the anticipation building with each passing second. As the minutes ticked by, the kitchen filled with an intoxicating aroma of baking.

The timer rang, and Andy removed the tray from the oven. The cookies were a vision of perfection, their rich chocolate chips glistening like jewels. She allowed them to cool for a few minutes on the baking sheet before transferring them to a wire rack.

Jackie couldn't resist grabbing one while it was still warm. The chocolate chips were gooey, and the cookie was delightfully chewy.

It was pure bliss in every bite.

Over the course of the next couple of hours, Jackie and Andy would welcome each of the house guests, one at a time, to partake in the cookies and discuss their whereabouts during the previous evening's blackout. Most importantly, during the theft of the Christmas Diamond.

MARGARET

As the matriarch entered and sat, the lodge's wood paneled dining room filled with a chill even colder than the wintery mountain air outside.

"Cookie?" Jackie asked her friend, showing the platter on the table.

"I had breakfast, thank you." Margaret replied.

"Don't mind if I do." Jackie said, sampling Andy's handiwork. She smiled. While her onetime protégé might well turn out to be a jewel thief, she certainly *knew* how to bake a good cookie.

"They're my mother's recipe," Jackie explained. "She had a secret ingredient."

"Finally!" Jackie smiled. "A case I can really sink my teeth into!"

"I don't suppose you could tell me *why* you wanted them?" Andy asked.

"All in good time, my young apprentice." Jackie smiled, turning back to Margaret. "Please. Take us through what happened."

"Well, after game night ended, I went to my study to put the diamond back in the safe," she recalled. "I dialed in the combination and opened the door. The next thing I knew, it went dark. I tried the light switch, but nothing worked."

"Because someone cut the power." Jackie added.

"Exactly!" Margaret said, shooting Andy an accusatory stare. "*Someone* did. Anyway, by the time the lights came back on, the Christmas Diamond was missing. Taken from the safe under my nose!"

"You were watching the safe the entire time?" Jackie asked.

"Not the entire time, no. Like I said, I tried the light switch." Margaret remembered.

"Which means your back was turned for what, three, four seconds?"

"Maybe a little more."

"Oh?" Jackie raised an eyebrow. Andy leaned forward. Had Jackie caught the woman in a lie?

"Well, when the switch didn't work, I tried the lamp on my desk."

"So how long would you say your back was turned to the safe?" Jackie continued.

"A minute?" Margaret estimated.

"During that minute anything could have happened." Jackie did the math in her head.

"Something did happen. My diamond was stolen." Margaret blurted out, "By her!"

"Allegedly." Jackie reminded her.

"Is this a court?" Margaret scoffed. "Are we on trial? There's no presumption of innocence. No, just a suitcase, *belonging* to her, found in *her room*, with *my diamond* in it."

"If that's true, then I will prove it." Jackie noted.

"But it's not!" Andy protested.

"Then I will prove *that*," Jackie grinned.

"Fine," Margaret shot back. "You want to waste your Christmas playing these stupid reindeer games, be my guest. But I've told you everything I know. If you don't mind, I'll be going."

"Sure you won't have a cookie?" Andy tried to extend an olive branch.

"Very." Margaret said, snapping the olive branch in half, throwing it to the ground, and stomping on it for good measure.

UNCLE GARY

Chomping down on one of Andy's cookies after another, Gary recalled being in the living room when the power went out, before leaving with Liam. After all, it had been *his* request for an espresso that led Andy to go into the kitchen.

"Liam and I had gone to look for the circuit breaker." Gary recalled, crunching down on a mouthful of cookie, "He went upstairs while I went to the basement. Naturally I found it. I mean, a circuit breaker upstairs? Really? And my sister said *her* side of the family got all the brains?"

"You seem to know a lot about fuses." Jackie observed.

"Well, I'm in charge of the Christmas lights every year," Gary boasted. "Believe me, I know a thing or two about fuses."

Andy remembered seeing him outside when she'd first arrived, so he wasn't lying about that. He then reached for another cookie, believing that he'd cooperated enough. "Mind if I take some more for the road?"

"Actually, there is *one thing* I'm curious about," Andy interrupted him.

Gary looked up, his hand frozen just above the platter of cookies. He grew uncomfortable.

"That afternoon," Andy remembered. "I saw you and your wife in the foyer, fighting about your sister. Something about a *killer offer* you'd made?"

"What about it?" The unflappable Gary grew nervous.

"What was the offer?"

"Real estate stuff. You wouldn't understand," he sneered.

"I'm assuming then," Andy replied, "that *Margaret* didn't understand either?"

"Oh, she understood. She just enjoys being difficult. As I'm assure you've noticed." Gary said, before turning to Jackie, as if just remembering her friendship with Margaret, "No offense."

Jackie, however, just flashed an amiable smile. "None taken."

Gary sighed, letting his familial frustrations get the best of him. "She'll learn her lesson one day."

"You have to admit. Taking one of her most treasured possessions would be a good way to do that, don't you think?" Jackie suggested.

"It would," Gary admitted, before realizing she had asked him one of those leading/loaded interrogation questions. "Unfortunately, my sister has a long list of people seeking retribution."

Jackie smiles. She knew Margaret well enough to know not only was he not exaggerating, but that he also had a good point. As he got up and went on his merry way, fueled by a sugar high from his snack, Andy hoped his wife Leonora might have even more information.

AUNT LEONORA

Unfortunately, Gary's wife Leonora wasn't any more forthcoming about that altercation from the previous afternoon.

"I wouldn't call it a fight," she shrugged. "We'd simply presented the woman with an opportunity for a new investment. Is it so wrong to want to share our good fortune with family?"

"Are you sure it was *her* good fortune you cared about?" Andy pressed.

"What are you suggesting?" Leonora bristled.

"Just trying to fill in details."

"Details?" Leonora jeered with condescension. "You wouldn't know the first thing about wealth management. Seriously! What's the point of all this? We *all* know what really happened! Personally, I wish the cops would just come and put an end to this ridiculous charade!"

"Do we *really* know?" Jackie asked. "Because I can't honestly say *I* do!"

Leonora sighed and crossed her arms. "Are we done?"

Jackie shook her head. "Let's skip ahead to later that night, shall we? After Bridgette spilled on you."

"I went to clean off my dress," Leonora replied with an impatient sigh. "Which, incidentally, she *completely ruined*. I ran into Harper in the kitchen. And we had the loveliest little *mother-daughter* chat."

"I remember that *lovely* chat." Andy recalled seeing Leonora and Harper shouting at each other. "It seemed pretty heated. Mind telling us what it was about?"

"It was about *none of your business*," Leonora replied with a haughty stare.

"Then where did you go?" Jackie jumped in to change the subject.

"You know darn well." Leonora snapped, remembering Jackie seeing her in the great room that evening. "And you know I was still there around the time the power went out."

"*Around* the time the power went out? Or *when* the power went out?"

"Does it matter?"

"It does to Margaret."

Insulted, Leonora stared daggers at Jackie so sharp that they might have drawn blood. "I think you and I both know; I had *nothing* to do with it. So, if you don't mind, I'm going to go now."

Leonora stood. And then, as if daring either Jackie or Andy to stop her, left in a huff. Jackie, however, wasn't concerned. After all, there were two sides to every story, and if one side wouldn't cooperate, she knew the other just might.

COUSIN HARPER

Harper sat at the table, nervous. The youngest of the group, she was used to being reprimanded at the finest educational institutions Kenilworth money could provide. This felt a lot like that, although she couldn't recall any of them ever having fresh cookies in their offices.

"Why were you and your mother fighting?" Jackie asked, dispensing with any illusion of pleasantry. She wanted to know the story behind the disagreement that Andy had witnessed.

"I'd told my mother I'm not going to France with the university," Harper sighed before clarifying: "I mean I *am* going. Just not for school."

Jackie smiled, and leaning forward, dropped her voice to a soothing whisper. It reminded Andy of yet another tool in the interrogator's tool kit. Gain the suspect's trust. *Come on,* the interrogator might say. *Just between us. I promise.*

"Whatever you have to say," Jackie said in a soft, placating voice, "stays in this room."

Harper opened up. In fact, the youngest guest of the party even blushed. "His name is Cedric. He'd come over as part of an exchange program last semester. Like I told my mother, he's handsome, very educated. Comes from a great family. Uber rich."

"That night," Jackie leaned forward, "you told your mother you intended to drop out of school for the third time?"

"Fourth." Harper admitted. "I begged her not to tell daddy. Especially not tonight. He has enough on his plate."

"You mean with his... exciting new endeavor?" Jackie asked.

"Yeah, right." Harper scoffed sarcastically. "His *new endeavor.*"

"How did your mother take the news?" Jackie already knew about the argument Andy witnessed between Harper and her mother, but she wanted to hear it from the young girl's own mouth.

"Not well." Harper recalled. "And Aunt Margaret threatened to cut off my inheritance! Just because I was seeing, and I quote, *a commoner.*"

Andy wasn't surprised. It was perhaps the most *Margaret-esque* thing to say. But what surprised her was that she'd directed it to a member of her own family. "A little harsh, isn't it?"

"Indeed." Jackie agreed before asking Harper, "And where were you during the black out?"

"Out in the courtyard." Harper replied. "Texting Cedric."

"On your other phone?" Jackie asked.

"Yes." Harper sighed with guilt. Then, pulling out that second phone, she held it for both Jackie and Andy to see. "Look if you don't believe me."

The girl was telling the truth. The two could read the text exchange, with the matching date and time stamps. According to the messages, she'd been telling Cedric about her upcoming trip. And Cedric was jealous because he'd never been.

"Did anyone else see you?" Jackie asked.

"That weird French guy. With the tats."

"The chef." Jackie nodded, recognizing the description. "Your mother isn't exactly a fan."

"My mother isn't a fan of anything," Harper laughed.

"And you were both there when the power went out?" Jackie asked her.

Harper nodded.

"Thank you," Jackie said to Harper as she stood. "And don't worry, we won't say a word about Cedric."

Harper sighed with relief and got up to leave.

LIAM

Liam couldn't remember the last time he was tongue tied. Maybe it was that seventh-grade field trip when he had to share a bus bench with Jenny Flynn on the way to the local art museum. Or maybe the time he had to recite the infamous "Friends, Romans, Countrymen" monologue from "Julius Caesar" for his 10th grade English class, proving once and for all that he would never be an actor. But he sat at the table in front of Jackie and Andy and was absolutely speechless. It could have been the nerves. It could have been the weariness from an exhausting evening. Or... perhaps it was Andy, who was radiant in the light of the tree and not at all like someone who was about to interrogate him...

"Yoo hoo," Jackie whistled, interrupting his rambling thoughts. "Over here."

Blushing, Liam turned to Jackie. "Sorry. It's just... it's kind of exciting. This is my first interrogation. Not that it's a... you know what I mean."

"Just walk us through what happened last night," Jackie replied.

"Not much to tell. Andy left the room to make coffee, the power went out, and Uncle Gary and I went to look for the fuse box."

"You didn't know where it was?" Jackie asked, puzzled.

"Mother always had people that took care of stuff like that," Liam answered, feeling a little embarrassed.

"Uh huh." Jackie scribbled in her pad.

Liam froze. As if just recognizing the motive behind her question. "Wait. Are you asking if *I* had something to do with... what happened?"

"Did you?"

"No." Liam grew defensive. "And even if I *was* going to take it, why would I do it last night, when the house was full of guests? I could've gone into her study *any* time."

"Good point," Jackie nodded.

"Did anyone actually <u>see</u> you go upstairs?" Andy then asked.

Liam suddenly grew quiet. Something both Jackie and Andy noticed. Before he replied. "No. There was no one else up there."

AMELIA

"He's lying." Amelia blurted during her own questioning. "*I saw him up there.*"

"You were in your room?" Jackie asked.

"I went upstairs. I was feeling tired, and I wanted to lie down."

"Why do you suppose he didn't mention it?" Jackie asked.

Amelia turned to Andy with a snide giggle. "Probably because he wanted to spare *her* feelings. You didn't really think it takes *that long* to look for a circuit breaker, did you? I didn't come back down until *after* the power came back. When Margaret screamed."

Andy scowled. The thought of Liam, the handsome boy she'd crushed on all those years ago, sharing himself with *this* woman was almost unthinkable. Worse even was the fact that Amelia seemed aware of Andy's feelings and seemed to relish hurting them.

"What were you and Liam doing?" Jackie asked.

"A lady doesn't kiss and tell." Amelia replied, giving Andy a grin.

"Then it's a good thing you're not a lady." Jackie replied.

"Excuse me?" the heiress said with indignance.

"A true lady doesn't enjoy toying with someone's emotions." Jackie smiled. "However, a child might."

"I'm afraid I don't care for your tone," Amelia scoffed.

"How'd you meet?" Jackie shot back.

"Is that relevant?" Amelia asked.

"Two of the wealthiest families in California, if not the country, on track for a merger until the deal falls apart and a priceless treasure goes missing in the process?" Jackie said in a mouthful. "Yes, I'd say it is."

"Why, you make it sound like a business deal," Amelia noted.

"Well, it *was*, wasn't it?" Jackie snapped back. "The question is why Amelia Vanderkamp would be so interested in Liam Kenilworth."

"We have so much in common," Amelia started before Jackie interrupted again.

"You have *absolutely nothing* in common," the writer observed.

"If you think I did all of that just so I could get a diamond…"

"You did all of that because your family's fortune is dwindling, and you wanted something far more important to you than Liam Kenilworth." Jackie smiled. "You wanted Liam Kenilworth's *money*. The diamond was just a consolation prize."

"May I remind you, I was…" Amelia smiled before continuing, "*indisposed* at the moment Margaret's beloved bauble went missing. And I have a witness to that fact."

Jackie just stared. Andy realized the whole confrontation had been a ruse to test Amelia's steely resolve.

"Hope I was of some help," Amelia said, feigning regret. "It's always hard to see something so horrible happen to someone… *so close*."

With Amelia's departure from the room, the interrogations had ended. Jackie and Andy stood there for a moment in silence. They had plenty of information to ponder. Jackie spoke.

"Your turn."

ANDY

Finally, it had come down to just the two of them. Andy and Jackie. The family had all passed through without Jackie finding a solution, and she was curious what her would-be protégé might contribute.

None of this came as any surprise to Andy. She'd expected her turn to answer questions, and knew she had nothing to hide. The truth would be on her side, and that, in the real world, was all that mattered. Except this was not the real world. This was the Kenilworths' world. And in the Kenilworths' world, the concept of truth was always flexible.

"As you recall," Jackie said, pacing the room in deep thought. "You made me a bet."

"Yes, I did." Andy nodded.

"You've heard the witness testimonies."

"I have."

"You know the accusations others have made, including the fact that they found the evidence in your possession."

"Yes."

"So now," Jackie said, remembering the wager the two had made earlier in the evening, where Andy promised to find inconsistencies in the accusations against her. "*Three holes.*"

Andy took a moment. And a deep breath. Then she spoke. "Hole one. Assuming the witnesses' timelines are accurate, there was no way I had enough time to take the necklace, hide it in my room, <u>and</u> get back to the kitchen."

"Unless you took the elevator."

"*Except,* the elevator runs on electricity. So I could never have taken it during the blackout."

"True." Jackie nodded, impressed.

"Hole two. While it's true, I *might* have had a motive," Andy paced. "I'm certainly not the only one. Lots of people besides me had an opportunity. We know who was in the great room. But we also know several guests *were not.* Amelia and Liam were upstairs doing... something. Harper was out back. Leonora was returning from the foyer."

"Do I hear three?" Jackie asked before Andy grew silent, which alarmed the detective.

"Look, Jackie," Andy began, dropping her voice.. "You know I'm one of your biggest fans. And the *last* thing I'd ever want to do is accuse you of *anything.*"

"Says the girl about to accuse me of something."

"But even *you* would have to admit that, lately you've been..." Andy started, reaching for the exact and delicate word to use, "*borrowing...* from some of your earlier works?"

"I'm listening."

"For instance," Andy explained, "I guessed the killer's identity in the 2nd chapter of *Murder at 30,000 Feet*, because it was the same motive and culprit as *Blood on...*"

"*... the Snow*," Jackie replied, surprised and impressed that a reader picked up on her creative shortcut. "You caught me."

"Of course, I'm referring to the book," Andy clarified, "Since the movie changed the killer's identity."

"They thought it'd be easier to get a name," Jackie defended the decision. "But I don't see the relevance."

"Well," Andy continued, "if we *are* borrowing from our past works... consider the plot *Fail Safe*."

Jackie leans back, understanding her point.

"A priceless jewel disappears from an heiress's safe?" Andy exclaimed, summing up the plot of one of her favorite books. "In the middle of a dinner party? As I recall, wasn't the twist in that book that the one who-done-it was the *detective* herself?"

"Three holes," Jackie nodded.

"You see?" Andy exhaled. "I didn't do it!"

"You poked three holes in my theory," Jackie admitted. "That doesn't mean you're innocent."

"Yeah." Andy sighed, disappointed.

But then, Jackie's face lit up like the Christmas tree sitting by the window. "Wait, I've got it!"

Andy breathed a sigh of relief. "You do?"

"It took me a while, but I did it!" Jackie grew more excited. "I've cracked the case!"

"What is it?" Andy asked.

"Black pepper," Jackie replied. "Your mother's secret ingredient in the cookie is black pepper."

Andy's smile faded, realizing Jackie was no closer to solving the one mystery that mattered most. "Yes, Jackie. Black pepper."

As Jackie took another cookie, Andy asked, "You never told me why you wanted them in the first place."

"Simple," came Jackie's reply. "A guilty party will always want something else to focus on. Helping them to sell their... *prevarication*."

"Such as, say, a plate of fresh baked cookies?" Andy nodded, figuring it out.

"Not to mention," Jackie giggled, shoveling in another cookie, "they taste much better than a polygraph!"

"Did it work?" Andy asked.

"Like a charm." Jackie grinning.

That's when they heard the ringing. *BRRRRRING*. It was almost like a bicycle bell, and the sharp, reverberating tone flooded the house. *BRRRRRING*.

It was the sound of a vintage telephone.

BRRRRING! The loud ringing was followed by footsteps, heels clacking loudly on the hardwood flooring, and then, by the lifting of a receiver. Andy and Jackie both listened. Was it related to the matter at hand?

"Yes?" They heard Margaret say into the phone, her voice carrying from a distant room. "Really? Okay, great. See you then."

Click. She hung up. And then, more footsteps. This time, growing closer. With both Jackie and Andy hanging in suspense, Margaret slid the ornate pocket doors open to the dining room. She stood there in the doorway, with that imposing stance and coy smile on her face that she'd become known for.

It was a smile Andy knew well. And she knew it always meant trouble.

"You'll be happy to know," Margaret announced, unable to contain her dark and twisted glee. "That was Detective Billings."

"I realize you're concerned," Jackie interrupted. "But if you'd just let me investigate a little while longer..."

"Lucky for you then," Margaret cut her off. "He's not able to stop by until tomorrow afternoon. At which time, he'll be taking statements personally, and probably..." Margaret turned to Andy, "...taking *you*. So, *I'm* not the one who should be concerned."

"Are you sure?" Andy protested. "Because I'm innocent. Which means whoever stole your diamond is still here! In this lodge!"

"Prove it," Margaret retorted. "Or the only piece of jewelry you'll be getting this Christmas... *will be a pair of handcuffs*!"

CHAPTER FIVE

Tibb's Eve, also known as "Tipsy Eve" or "Tibb's Evening," was a term used in Newfoundland and Labrador, Canada, to refer to the night of December 23rd. It was a time for friends and family to gather and celebrate prior to the more formal Christmas celebrations of December 24th and 25th. It was a night where friends and family would gather for drinks, snacks, and general merriment.

This was December 23rd. Tibb's Eve. The sun had already gone to sleep for the night, and Andy was exhausted from hours of straight interrogation. As she trudged into the foyer from the dining room, Liam approached her with a smile. And a glass.

"Our famous Kenilworth spiced ale," Liam said as he handed the reddish-brown cocktail to Andy. "Mother has it made special every Tibb's Eve."

"Is it alcoholic?"

"Very," he grinned.

With that, she downed it in one gulp.

"I'm guessing you didn't have any luck solving the case?" he asked, sensing her weariness.

"Honestly?" Andy sighed, "I'm a little light on motives."

"How about I walk you to your room and we can talk about it?"

He was about to walk her out, but she stopped dead in her tracks. There was a question on her mind. She needed an answer.

"Why didn't you say you saw Amelia upstairs?" she asked.

"What did she tell you?"

"Enough," she replied, refusing to let her imagination fill in the blanks.

"Andy," his eyes pleaded, even if his words were no more reliable than the lies he'd told earlier, "*nothing happened.*"

Andy stared into his face. That adorable smile that she'd wanted to kiss so badly so many times. She wanted to believe him. *Desperately.* Yet, despite her growing attraction, she knew she couldn't. Not yet, anyway.

"I'll walk you," came Jackie's voice, as the author strode up. Andy was saved by the bell.

"See you," was all Andy could muster as she followed Jackie upstairs for the night.

Returning to the guest room she shared with Margaret's collection of figurines, Andy had never felt less welcome. Not even Jackie, sensing her discomfort, could calm her. Ordinarily, she'd look forward to throwing on some comfortable pajamas and curling up with a good book. Perhaps even one written by Jackie herself. Now, all she could imagine was a house full of unfriendly, haughty strangers all talking about her behind her back.

"Why do I feel like a prisoner?" she sighed, turning to Jackie.

"It's not like you're locked up." Jackie pointed out.

"I might as well be." Andy thought, remembering the phone call they'd overheard. "That detective is coming tomorrow!"

"Just try to get some sleep, okay?" Jackie suggested.

"Jackie?" Andy looked up as the author stood halfway out the door. "You believe me, don't you?"

Jackie smiled. "Three holes," she said before adding, "Good night."

She closed the door. Andy turned, alone in the room, and sauntered over to her luggage. Compared to the matching sets she'd watched her housemates wheel in, with their damier and check patterns, her rolling duffel bag from Walmart felt even cheaper than it already was. She grabbed a pair of sweats to sleep in and then, snapped off the lamp.

That's when she glimpsed someone! Standing outside the window!

She froze! And did a quick double take! Whatever prowler she *thought* she saw, silhouetted against the moonlit snow, was gone.

'TWAS TWO NIGHTS BEFORE Christmas when all through the estate,

> *Not a Kenilworth was stirring, not Gary, nor his mate*
> *The diamond had been returned to the safe with care*
> *With hopes that Detective Billings soon would be there*

However, not quite *everyone* was asleep in their 'kerchiefs and caps, with visions of sugarplums dancing in their heads. The floorboards groaned under the weight of two feet, wearing simple tennis shoes, as Andy's door creaked open! A blade of light sliced through the room as the ominous silhouette entered. Dressed in a black hoodie and black pants, the Stranger examined Andy's things with a gloved hand. Her clothes. Her toiletries.

Meanwhile, Andy lay in bed fast asleep, unaware of the violation that was taking place.

The Stranger hovered over her, staring.

Then, they made their move.

THE SUN CRESTED THE mountains, the puffy pink clouds reflecting on the glassy surface of icy Lake Tahoe below. It was December 24th. Christmas Eve.

As Andy's eyes opened, she turned to the window. It surprised her she'd slept as soundly as she did. Each passing minute brought the detective closer to her door, and Andy wasn't any closer to solving the crime. She knew she looked guilty, and she imagined that, if the roles were reversed, she'd suspect herself too.

However, turning in the bed, she noticed that the door was ajar. She remembered Jackie had closed it the night before. Someone must have opened the door after she'd fallen asleep! But why?

The answer came soon enough. A holiday card sat on her bedside table just beneath the lamp. Her name, Andy, was typed right on the front. Seizing the envelope, she ripped into it, eager to find any clue that might explain what had happened.

The card itself was generic, the type that would have been sold in a package of twenty at the store. There was a colorful cartoon of a reindeer accompanied by a pun. "Oh deer, Christmas is here." Inside, however, was one of the suspect cards from that mystery board game, *Whodunit*. The classic illustration on the yellowed card depicted a burglar with a black eye mask, stealing a pastry off a food tray.

Andy had just pulled the card for *The Thief*.

BY THE TIME JACKIE made her way down to the kitchen for breakfast, she was starving. Her usual cookies wouldn't be enough to hold herself over this morning. She'd spent so much time the previous day trying to help Andy that she'd neglected her own appetite. Hunger, however, took a back seat as she noticed something unusual. Not that Bridgette was the one cooking, but that the *actual* chef was nowhere to be found.

"No Raphael this morning?" Jackie asked, curious.

"He didn't come down," Bridgette explained. "But don't worry. How would you like your eggs?"

"Soft scrambled, please." Jackie said. She wandered to the window and noticed Andy was already outside.

It was on that back porch, in the crisp morning air, that Andy let Olivia in on what had happened the previous night. Olivia held the card and envelope in her hand, torn between concern for her friend and solidarity with the family that had turned against her.

"I figure," Andy said, mulling over the possibilities. "It's someone who's trying to threaten me or..."

"Or *what*?" Olivia blurted out.

"Help me." Andy replied. Which, no matter how mysterious or off-putting it appeared, was still more welcome than Olivia's current suspicions. In fact, Olivia could only scoff at Jackie's theory.

"Come on," Andy pleaded. "We've known each other how long? Do you *really* think I could steal from anyone? All I want is a chance to prove my innocence."

"I admit," Olivia said, softly. "I... might have rushed a little in doubting you."

"*Doubted what, exactly*?" came an older voice from out of sight. Andy knew it was Margaret. There was never a sunny moment this woman was incapable of casting a shadow over. Andy, not wanting to draw her into a conversation, hid the card.

"Perhaps you two were in on it together!" Margaret said in her usual, accusatory tone.

Olivia just rolled her eyes. "Must you always assume the worst?"

"That's for Captain Billings to figure out."

That's when Andy noticed Liam walk by. He looked away. No doubt he was having second thoughts about the day before, but unlike the rest of the family, he seemed contrite. Still, as sorry as he was, the image of him and Amelia together mere hours earlier was more than Andy wanted to imagine.

Margaret picked up on their energy. "You can play your little games with me," she muttered to Andy, "But you mess with *my son*... and you will witness a side of me you'll wish you never saw." Then, with a sneer and a glee about having salt to rub into Andy's wound, "Besides... he's already spoken for. By someone far more worthy of his affections than you!"

As Margaret stormed away, Andy turned to the card. With her own name staring back at her, typed on the envelope, a light bulb went off in her head.

"Does your family own a typewriter?"

THE FIRST TYPEWRITER that Frederick Kenilworth purchased was The Williams 1, manufactured by Domestic Sewing Machine Company in 1891. An early curved keyboard model, it had glass key tops and decorated frames. Soon after, other models would follow as Mr. Kenilworth quickly expanded his collection. These included the Crandall New Model, manufactured by the Crandall Machine Company in 1886, impressively detailed with its mother-of-pearl inlay and hand-painted floral arrangements; the Remington Number 1, produced by E. Remington and Sons in 1874, and the very model which Mark Twain used to become the first author to submit a typewritten manuscript; and the crème de la crème: the Rasmus Mailing-Hansen Writing Ball from 1870, unique for its arrangement of 52 keys on a large brass hemisphere.

Mr. Kenilworth had placed them on display back when the home office was his intellectual man cave, and neither his widow Margaret, nor children Olivia and Liam, had the heart to put them into storage when he'd passed away. As a result, they'd been there ever since, only being removed from their protective glass cases once a month to be cleaned.

Until now, that is. Andy carefully lifted the glass on the first one.

"I don't see what you're hoping to prove," Olivia said, wincing.

"I'll let you know when I finish," Andy replied with confidence. She slid the paper in.

"Have you even used one of these before?" Olivia asked.

"My grandmother had a Casio when I was like 10." Andy contributed, without dispelling any of Olivia's fears.

Thunk. Thunk. The heavy letter sprung forth as Andy pressed a key. She then spun the wheel, *ziiiiiiiiiip*, removed the paper and moved to the next typewriter in the collection. *Thunk. Thunk. Ziiiiiiiiiip.* Rinse, wash, repeat.

Olivia found her eyes turning to the door, wondering what Margaret might say if she caught Andy touching her late husband's prized collection. After all, you couldn't kick someone out of the house if they're already on house arrest. Perhaps she'd confine her to her room. She decided it would be best to lock the door. *Better to ask for forgiveness than permission*, she reasoned. Especially if your mother was the sort to make Cruella DeVil look as cuddly as the puppies she craved.

Thunk. Thunk. Ziiiiiiiiiip.

"Winner winner, chicken dinner," Andy announced, showing the Crandall.

"Okay, you got me," Olivia said, confused.

Andy pointed at the envelope. "Look at the top of the A in my name. See the impression?" She then pressed the "A" key on the Crandall. *Thunk.* It created similarly flawed lettering on her test paper. "Whoever sent that card, most likely our thief, used *this* typewriter!"

"Any idea who?" Olivia asked, hope rising in her voice.

"Someone who had access to this room. And this typewriter."

"In other words, pretty much everyone in this lodge."

Andy's eyes narrowed. "Where does your mother keep the key to this room?"

"All the doors unlock with one primary key. She has one. I'm sure the staff has a copy."

An idea occurred to Andy. "You know, there is *one person* we didn't talk to last night. Someone who conveniently seems to be missing this morning. Someone on the staff."

"Who?" Olivia asked.

"Let's find out." Andy replied, her eyes falling upon Margaret's dinosaur of a home computer.

While Andy wasn't as proficient as Liam, the computer was the same model, with its then-high-tech Pentium 4 processor, as the one she'd had as a little girl, when she'd played old games like *The Sims* with her brother. This meant she knew enough to navigate the directory. While the computer's own security would have presented a formidable challenge, the matriarch kept her computer's password on a piece of paper helpfully taped to the side of the monitor. In bold. And size 20 font.

"Okay, here we go," Andy said, jumping to the date and time in question and hitting play.

Sure enough on screen, the two women could make out Harper, sitting alone, texting on her phone, just as she recounted during her conversation. Then, confirming her story, Raphael came out and placed a phone call. The girl barely paid him any attention.

"Little Miss Entitled was telling the truth," Olivia said, surprised.

"Now, let's fast forward to the blackout." Andy hit fast forward. With Harper's face still buried in her phone, they notice Raphael... *walking back into the lodge.*

"Wait..." Olivia's eyes narrowed. Sure enough, not one minute later, the blackout took place. The entire video feed went dark. After all, the blackout would have also affected the cameras as well.

"Raphael went inside before the blackout!" Andy gasps.

"He had time to cut the power and steal the diamond!" Olivia noted.

"And of course, now he's missing." Andy sighed.

"He couldn't have gone far!" Olivia exclaimed, "We have to find him!"

THE DOOR TO THE KITCHEN burst open and Andy and Olivia charged in. Neither had expected Raphael to *be* there, although there was the *slightest* chance he could have been, hunkered over the stove preparing a croque madame for lunch. Alas, the kitchen was empty. Bridgette had even cleaned up after making breakfast, so it was both empty *and* spotless. Olivia then turned to a series of hooks on the wall. There were some keys there, helpfully labeled. In bold. And size 20 font.

Garden shed. Cellar door.

But one hook was empty.

Gate opener.

They heard a car engine revving outside! Andy and Olivia exchanged frantic glances!

Raphael had always been proud of his native country. Which was why, while his wealthy, fellow award winners in the food industry gravitated towards more traditional automobiles, such as the BMW, Raphael turned to a *Gallic* clone, the DLC Roadster produced by the French manufacturer De La Chapelle.

And now that Roadster was speeding towards the gate. Raphael reached down and pulled out the opener. The one missing from the hook. He pressed the button.

The gate swung open. Just beyond it lay the mountain road, which wound down the side of snow-covered Monument Peak towards the lake below, a road that would lead to freedom. He was almost there. His foot pressed the pedal to the floor as his hand shifted, throwing the tiny roadster into top gear.

But a tiny frame jumped in front of the gate! It was Olivia. Waving frantically. Their eyes locked in a standoff. With little time to brake, and realizing the scrappy yet powerful roadster would not stop on a *franc*, Raphael realized he'd have to choose. Olivia or the gate. The car would hit one.

He swerved, plowing his beloved car headlong into the iron fence. Dizzy from the impact, Raphael pried himself out and continued his escape on foot. While the car's chassis crumpled in the collision, the fortified fence remained intact. With Olivia racing in his direction, Raphael pivoted, making a split-second decision to disappear into the estate's vast backyard.

Inside the lodge's foyer, Gary clamored down the stairs. Harper raced down the hall in his direction.

"What's going on?" Gary demanded to know. "What's all the racket?"

"The chef!" Harper turned away from the window, having witnessed the slapdash pursuit pass by. "He's on the run!"

That was all Gary needed to hear. He turned and made a beeline for the great room. Leonora followed, just in time to see him grab the antique flintlock off the mantle. Who knew if it would even fire? But that was always Gary's way. Shoot first and ask questions later. Only this time, that was *literally* what he was about to do.

"Gary! What are you doing?!" Leonora exclaimed.

"Margaret, check upstairs!" Gary shouted. "I'm going out back!"

The estate's property covered five acres, leading right up to the edge of the mountain. It was covered in snow, which made Raphael's attempted escape more ridiculous. Trying to flee while trudging through the thick, icy slush was a bit like trying to race through quicksand. Yet Raphael was going to give it the old *l'université* try.

"Where'd he go?" Gary shouted, racing outside.

Liam, who'd heard the car crash, came running, only to watch Raphael traipse past. But then Gary, in close pursuit, tripped in the snow. He fell, landing onto the rifle. It fired... *something*. The shrapnel barely missed Liam, shattering the bark on a nearby tree!

"Was that a musket?" he asked incredulously.

Andy, nearly witnessing her would-be beau meet an ignominious end at the hands of a century old howitzer, rushed to his side.

Meanwhile, Leonora, recognizing that her careless husband was only one misstep away from involuntary manslaughter, grabbed the weapon from his hands.

"You could have hurt someone!" she scolded.

The only thing that the infamous Christmas Musket Incident, as they would later call it, had caused *was Raphael's clean escape*. Because by the time the proverbial musket dust settled, the epicurean felon was nowhere to be found.

IN A SOCIETY WHERE the upper one percenters try to outdo each other with the real estate equivalent of phallometrics, size means everything. After all, who *wouldn't* want a home kitchen spacious enough to cater a guest list in the high three digits. However, the problem with keeping up with the Joneses is that, in this case, it meant there were *so* many places for a fugitive to hide, not even *Indiana* Jones could find him.

Harper and Leonora took to searching the garage and driveway. Bridgette wound her way through the maze of boxes that comprised much of the lodge's basement. Margaret and Gary were upstairs on the sizable second floor, going from room to room. Besides the primary bedroom, there were also four guest rooms, five bathrooms, a craft room, a gym room, a panic room, a game room, and something called a hearth room, but not even Margaret knew what that meant.

Olivia, upon returning the rifle to its rightful place above the fireplace, conducted her own search on the first floor. Jackie helped as they scoured the foyer, kitchen, dining room, great room, den, and home theater, where Amelia had been entertaining herself with an episode of the Real Housewives instead of helping.

Andy and Liam, meanwhile, conducted their own search down by the pool. Covered for the winter, the area, with its outdoor kitchen, pool house, and pool shed, offered more than its fair share of hiding places.

"If he *is* innocent, he's doing a terrible job convincing us." Liam noted, before lowering his voice. "Look. About last night..."

"We're both adults," Andy interrupted. "It doesn't matter."

"It *does* matter," Liam protested. "Because *nothing* happened."

Andy stopped. "Tell me something. And I want the *truth*, okay?"

Liam studied her for a moment, wondering where this was headed before uttering, "I promise."

"How much money do you owe?" she asked.

"Wow," Liam sighed. "I didn't see that coming."

"Can't help it. I love a good mystery."

"How did you know?"

She remembered back to when they'd first encountered each other a couple of days ago in the foyer. When he'd dropped his newspaper opened to the sports page, with particular scores circled with a marker.

"When we first met," Andy recalled, channeling her idol Jackie's talent for deductive reasoning. "You were carrying a newspaper open to the sports pages. You circled certain scores. I'm guessing for bets you'd placed. Also, you were having a heated conversation on the phone with someone you most likely owed money to. And you must admit, you make everything a wager."

Liam sighed. There was no point in denying it anymore. He knew she'd figured him out.

"Hundred fifty thousand. Give or take."

"I hate to say it," Andy said, "but I just found your motive. So please be honest. What were you *really* doing upstairs during the blackout?"

"Well, um..." Liam started. "Like I said, I'd gone upstairs to look for the breaker panel."

"But..." Andy started. There was *always* a but.

"I noticed Amelia was in her room," Liam admitted. "So, I went to see her."

"If nothing happened...?" Andy started, her curiosity deepening with each passing second.

"I went to talk to her because I wanted to remind her it was over between us," Liam admitted. "In fact, I told her I wanted her to go home!"

"And?"

"She said she would. Until mother locked the place down like her own little *Xanadu Alcatraz*." He looked up at Andy with his wide, brown pleading eyes. "That's all, I swear."

She stopped walking and turned towards him. They locked eyes. Perhaps there would be a future here between these two after all. Only time would tell. But the moment wouldn't last. Because at *that moment...*

...came another ear-splitting shriek! However, unlike before, this one was pained. Something bad had happened. And the voice was unmistakable.

"That sounded like my mother!" Liam exclaimed before the two raced for the house.

By the time they reached the foyer, Andy and Liam found Bridgette standing over a semi-conscious Margaret, lying at the bottom of the stairs. Olivia and Gary stood off to the side, watching over the scene with concern.

With this one harrowing development, Andy realized that her case just graduated from attempted theft to *attempted murder*!

CHAPTER SIX

Detective Paul Billings hated Christmas. It wasn't so much that he hated the holiday itself. After all, he'd dutifully attended the midnight Christmas Eve candlelight service ever since he was a child in upstate New York. And, as a young man just starting out in the NYPD, he and his bride-to-be had spent many afternoons strolling along Fifth Avenue, admiring the lights and decorations. What he hated was the fact that he was now expected to host a motley crew of family members every year. They threatened to turn his home into the holiday equivalent of Grand Central Station during what should be a time of peaceful rest. There were, of course, his grown son and daughter, their spouses, and their children. But inevitably, there would be a cousin or two, maybe an uncle, or some hungry neighbor whose own holiday plans fell apart at the last minute. Detective Billings knew his wife had a penchant for adopting lonely neighbors the way others might collect stray animals.

At least, he reasoned, as he pulled his family's SUV into the parking lot of the South Lake Tahoe Safeway for the second time that day, *he wasn't Margaret Kenilworth*. After all, who would ever want to host *that* brood?

Two minutes later, his phone rang.

Someone had shoved Margaret Kenilworth down the stairs.

By the time Paul Billings showed up at the Kenilworth estate, a near-vertical trek which, thanks to the increased snowfall that year, would test the most resilient of snow chains, investigators had already started combing through the lodge. He had brushed off the first call from the home, something about a necklace that was stolen, and had even considered letting someone else take this case altogether. Still, he knew Margaret, being a longtime friend and contributor to the police fund, would demand his presence. A purloined piece of jewelry was one thing. Attempted murder would be another.

Billings made his way through the lodge to find Margaret on the couch in the great room. There she laid, surrounded by the comforting holiday trappings and holding a bag of frozen brussels sprouts against her bruised forehead. Olivia stood by her side.

"How are you feeling?" Billings asked, leaning down to tend to his injured friend.

"Like I fell down the stairs," she said with a wry smile. Nothing could deprive the woman of her cynical sense of humor.

"I was told someone *pushed* you?" Billings asked.

"All I know is," she replied with exasperation. "One minute I was at the top of the stairs, looking for Raphael, and the next, I'm down here, lying on the floor, and my head is pounding."

Olivia wasn't about to give up. "My mother went up and down those stairs a hundred times a day. I'm telling you, *someone did this.*"

"Either way," Billings said, looking beneath the bag of frozen vegetables to note some significant bruising and swelling on the side of her head. "You need to go get that looked at. That's not a request, Margaret. Better safe than sorry."

The family then watched as paramedics loaded their matriarch into the back of an ambulance. If there was any hope that their troubles, having begun with the disappearance of a rare diamond, would soon be over... it died the moment the ambulance doors slammed shut.

With Margaret being tended to by the finest physicians Tahoe's Barton Memorial Hospital offered, Billings now turned to figuring out how she landed there. That would mean interrogating the family to investigate each of their whereabouts at the time of the injury.

"We were looking for Raphael," Olivia explained.

"We think he's the one that took the diamond." Liam said.

"*You* think he's the one that took the diamond," Amelia scoffed.

"Give it a rest, Amelia," Olivia rolled her eyes.

"Do you know what you get when you allow vermin into your house?" Amelia suggested in a haughty, condescending tone. "*An infestation*."

"*Either way*," Harper interjected, "The cook's been missing ever since."

Billings was scribbling copious notes. Keeping up with the various Kenilworth theories and motives could have kept an entire police department busy, let alone one detective.

"First, he's a chef, not a cook. And a very well-regarded chef at that." Bridgette defended him. "Second, Raphy would never hurt anyone!"

"Unless you count food poisoning," Leonora said with an arrogant grin. "Besides, he's not the *only* one around here with a motive to hurt Margaret, is he?"

"Go on," Billings asked.

"Margaret fired *her*." Leonora said, pointing her finger in Bridgette's direction.

"And *rehired* her." Olivia said, speaking up in her defense.

"Provisionally." Leonora shot back.

"The maid, the chef, I think it's clear that *whoever* is responsible is an outsider." Amelia said, again turning to Andy. "Including this one."

"*I'm* an outsider," Jackie noted. "As are *you*."

"You know what I mean." Amelia crossed her arms again.

Liam had heard enough. "Andy couldn't have done it. She was with me when it happened."

"And where was that?" Billings asked, his hand working overtime trying to keep up.

"Down by the pool," Liam answered, tossing a sympathetic glance in Andy's direction.

"Doing what?" Amelia demanded, letting her envy show.

"Looking for Raphael!" Liam shot back, as if Amelia inferred anything else.

"Which was more than you were doing," Olivia said, remembering how she'd spotted Amelia in the home theater. "Which reality show were you watching, again?"

"The Real Housewives." Jackie replied with a smile.

"Let me guess," Olivia said. "*Career* research?"

Amelia enjoyed being the center of attention, but she most definitely hated being the butt of a joke. Not wanting to dig her hole any deeper, she bit her proverbial tongue and sat silently, stewing in her hatred.

"Anyone else have an alibi?" Billings asked.

"We were together outside." Leonora replied, indicating Harper.

"And Jackie and I were on the first floor searching." Olivia replied.

Billings turned to Gary. "And you?"

"I was upstairs with my sister."

"Can anyone confirm that?"

"I suppose my sister would," Gary stated. "If someone hadn't pushed her down the stairs!"

More telling was the answer to Billings' final question, which he'd posed to each of the family members, one at a time. "Can anyone think of someone who wanted to harm Margaret?"

"My sister?" Gary scoffed.

"I think a better question would be..." Jackie started with a smile.

"...who *didn't*?" Andy said.

IF LIAM WAS HOPING the security camera would help find whoever had pushed Margaret, his optimism was soon dashed. The cameras had stopped recording just prior to the incident.

"Anything?" Andy asked him, hopeful.

"Someone stopped the recording," he sighed.

"Which means definitively... it wasn't an accident." Olivia realized.

"Right," Liam confirmed.

While it was possible that the computer could have simply *failed*, given its advanced age, it was more likely that someone stopped the recording manually. Unfortunately, there was no way to prove *who*. Especially since anyone with the ability to read a password printed in bold, size 20 font could have gained access to the computer. Moreover, the system was seemingly deactivated at some point *after* Raphael's short-lived road trip, which meant *anyone* could have taken advantage of the distraction. Perhaps even Raphael himself.

But then, before they could give the matter another thought, Andy and Liam heard a groan. It was the lodge's aging floorboards, and it came from down the hall, outside the office. But then, as the two peered out the office window, they saw everyone standing outside the window with Detective Billings, retracing their whereabouts from that afternoon.

So, if everyone else was outside the lodge *and* Margaret was laid up on the couch... who was making that noise?

Andy reasoned there was only one possibility.

Raphael was in the house.

LIAM EMERGED FROM THE home office, peering down the hallway. As Andy crept up behind him, he motioned for her to be quiet. The only thing they had going for them was the element of surprise. If *they* knew everyone else was outside, then it was safe to surmise that Raphael would assume the same. That meant he thought he was alone.

Creeeeeak. The floor groaned again. This time... it was coming from the kitchen! The two exchanged a nervous glance and continued onward.

Creeping into the kitchen, Liam didn't see any sign of Raphael. He seized a knife from the knife block and, motioning for Andy to stay quiet, began to make his way around the kitchen's vast island. Wielding that knife tight, he closed his eyes, took a deep breath, and then, he pounced!

"Got you!" he exclaimed.

That's when Raphael emerged! Only, he didn't wait for Liam to grab for him. He ran for it instead, back out into the hallway. Andy and Liam spun and raced after him.

"Hey!" Liam shouted, darting into the hall and launching himself into the fleeing chef. The two tussled as two of Billings' uniformed officers ran in from outside. Raphael was handcuffed and wrestled away.

At last, Raphael would face the *musique.*

THE KITCHEN, WHICH had been Raphael's domain during his tenure, was now, ironically, where Detective Billings would question him. Raphael sat at the kitchen table, his hands bound by handcuffs, watching Billings weave a case against him. Just a couple of days ago, he'd been using this table to prepare dinner. Now, it could be the last place he'd spend time as a free man.

But that's when Billings noticed Andy and Jackie enter. The other officers moved to keep them at bay, but they were persistent. Especially Jackie, whose reputation as a best-selling author had not gone unnoticed by Billings.

"Excuse me Detective, but I'm a crime writer..." she started.

"Jackie Evenson, yes." He finished her sentence with a smile. Such introductions were unnecessary when, as it turns out, his wife was a voracious reader.

"Actually, my wife insisted I get you to sign her book before I leave," Billings whispered with a smile.

"Gladly," Jackie said with a grin, motioning to Andy. "Provided you let *my assistant* and I observe?"

Billings pulled out two chairs. "Knock yourself out."

They all sat at the table with Raphael.

"Wolfgang Puck here was just about to tell me how he pushed Margaret down the stairs, isn't that right?" Billings asked.

"*Non, non!* I never laid a hand on Margaret!" Raphael exclaimed. "As for the night of the theft, *oui,* I was outside. I needed some air. After what that *woman* said about my work. Finally, I went back inside."

"And then the power mysteriously goes out." Billings remarked. "A little convenient, wouldn't you say?"

"Is it?" Raphael shrugged in his French-tinged, mangled English. "Is older house. Older wiring. I have to be careful with the appliances as it is."

"Is that when you stole the Christmas Diamond?" Billings went right for the jugular.

"Who, me?" Raphael was aghast at the accusation.

"Why not?" Billings replied. "Big shot like you, all the fame, all the accolades, it's gotta sting when someone like Leonora threatens your reputation. Sure you weren't looking for a little *payback*?"

At the back of the room, Jackie turned to Andy and whispered. "One victim, ten suspects. And, since everyone was split up, ten opportunities. I bet you a cookie that if the police questioned everyone, they'd find ten innocent people."

"Nine," Andy said, clarifying. "Nine innocent people. And *one liar*."

That's when Jackie stepped up to the chef and, to everyone's astonishment, spoke to him in fluent French.

"Raphael…" she started, "*vous dites que vous n'aviez rien à cacher.* <<You say you have nothing to hide.>>

"*C'est exact.*" <<That is correct.>>

"*Alors pourquoi avez-vous essayé de vous échapper?*" <<Then why did you try to escape?>>

"*J'ai dit que je n'avais fait de mal à personne. Je n'ai pas dit que je n'avais rien à cacher.*" <<I said I didn't hurt anyone. I never say I had nothing to hide.>>

"*Alors,*" Jackie replied, "*s'il vous plaît. Dites-leur la vérité.*" <<Then, please. Tell them the truth.>>

He hesitated. Her gentle request and calm demeanor earned his trust. So, he opened up. In English.

"For years I have been working with Margaret," Raphael replied. "Catering. Consultations. When the work became more consistent, she gave me access to funds to cover expenses. Business at the restaurant was not so good at first. I had to borrow money just to make ends meet."

"Let me guess," Billings intervened. "You didn't ask."

"I planned to pay it back before she knew it was even gone!" Raphael protested.

"And how much did you *borrow*?" Billings asked.

"Three, four hundred thousand. But that's why I went back into the house! To pay it back. Plus, interest!"

Raphael continued, growing more agitated. "I'm not stupid. I know what it looks like. My prints were on the safe. I had a motive. That's why I ran. Not because I stole a diamond. Certainly not because I hurt someone."

"And I'm supposed to believe that?" Billings asked. "After you *already* admitted you're a thief?"

He stood and read Raphael his Miranda rights. *You have the right to remain silent. Anything you say can be used against you.* But as the Detective spoke, something occurred to Andy. She checked the card she'd been sent just to be sure. Sure enough, she was right, and now she wanted to tell Jackie.

If you cannot afford a lawyer, one will be appointed for you.

"Look at this," Andy whispered, pulling out that envelope.

"That's the card, huh?" Jackie asked.

"Yes but look at it." Andy insisted. Jackie did. *The Thief.*

Do you understand the rights I have just read to you? With these rights in mind, do you wish to speak to me?

"I thought it was someone trying to *accuse* me," Andy whispered to Jackie. "But what if it was *a clue*? Look. This artwork, the thief, the food... and *Raphael*? That can't be a coincidence!"

"How did I not make that connection before? Very good work, Andy!"

"This means that someone on the inside," Andy started, "*knew his secret*!"

Less than seventy-two hours ago, the Kenilworths and their guests sat at the dining room table, listening to Leonora compare their dinner to automotive tires. Now, their host was recovering from a possible attempt on her life while that very same chef was being led out by police in handcuffs.

Watching from the lodge's front door, Olivia, Gary, Leonora stood with Andy and Jackie. The two exchanged a nervous glance as a sullen Raphael's head was pressed down to fit his tall, slender frame into the back of the cramped police cruiser. Then, they noticed yet another police car, pulling up the long driveway to the house.

Margaret Kenilworth had returned.

"Mother!" Olivia exclaimed at the sight of her mother, being escorted from the cruiser. Margaret had been called a great many things, ranging from arrogant to vindictive, petty and haughty, but never frail. Yet here she was, still shaken from the events of earlier that day, and showing each and every one of her advanced years in her weakened state.

"Do you know how many times I fell off my horse when I was little?" the matriarch huffed. "It's going to take more than a little tumble to break me! Still, under the circumstances, I've decided to cancel tomorrow's Christmas party."

Noticing that Detective Billings was about to get into the police car containing one Gallic gourmand, Gary stepped forth to stop him.

"So that's it, then?" Gary asked. "We can leave?"

"Gary!" Leonora hushed him.

He turned to the rest of the guests. "Oh, come on! You all saw! They caught the guy!"

"Not yet," Billings replied. "I'll be back in the morning to investigate the diamond incident."

"But it was returned!" Gary protested.

Olivia was having none of it. "Are you forgetting the part where someone tried to kill my mother?"

"Or, she slipped," Gary noted. "Accidents happen."

"Are you in a hurry?" Billings asked, sizing him up.

"As a matter of fact, I am," Gary stated. "I need to get back to the city and there's still time to grab the red eye."

"Unfortunately," Billing sighed. "I'm going to have to ask everyone to stick around. Including you, handsome."

Compared to this bunch, Billings looked *forward* to the family gathering that was awaiting him at home. He also knew his family would ask a hundred and one questions about this case. It seemed nothing got a family talking more than a police investigation on Christmas Eve.

And the same was true with the Kenilworths.

"Don't think this changes anything." Margaret said to Andy.

"Margaret, for crying out loud," Jackie exclaimed, growing tired of the endless accusations and suspicions of her young protégé. "They made an arrest!"

Margaret turned to Andy, lowering her threatening voice. "And until Captain Billings finishes his investigation, don't forget. I have cameras *all over this lodge.* Just in case you get any funny ideas about sneaking out in the middle of the night."

As the others piled inside to lavish attention on, not to mention grovel to, their recuperating host, Jackie just watched. Devouring her cookies like concessions in a theater. As Andy headed back inside, Jackie stopped her.

"I apologize." The writer said. "My friend seems to have a hard time accepting that you're off the hook."

"Do *you* think Raphael did it?" Andy asked.

"He had the opportunity. He had the motive."

"But do *you* think he did it?"

"A detective doesn't write the story," Jackie says, "they follow the story that the *evidence* tells them."

"What about *this* story?"

"I don't think it's over yet." Jackie said, heading back inside.

Andy sighed. She knew a thing or two about mystery fiction herself, and, in this case, she knew Jackie was right.

SOME PEOPLE TAKE SHOWERS in the morning when they wake up. Others take theirs in the evening before they go to bed. Andy had always been an evening person. Perhaps it was habitual from when she was growing up, when mornings in the house's sole bathroom were a bit like rush hour. Her mother and father would be trying to get ready for work while her brother prepared for a day of high school. A hot water tank could only hold so much, after all. Besides, her brother often used enough Axe body spray to disperse a minor riot, and no one dared go near the bathroom for at least an hour afterwards.

That evening, as night fell over the Kenilworth lodge, Andy took her customary evening shower. There she stood, enjoying the quality of water pressure only a house worth well over seven figures could provide, and singing.

"Up on the housetop, reindeer pause,
Out jumps good old Santa Claus."

What she didn't realize, as she enjoyed the acoustics, was that she was *not alone.*

"Down through the chimney with lots of toys,
All for the little ones, Christmas joys."

The door to the bathroom swung open, and the Stranger entered. It was the same person from the previous night. With the same black hoodie and black gloves. Reaching out with a similar card, the Stranger placed it on the bathroom counter, besides a large bottle of Margaret's melatonin gummies.

"Oh, who wouldn't go?
Who wouldn't go?"

Then, the Stranger disappeared through the door. Behind the shower door, shrouded in steam, Andy never knew they were there.

"Up on the housetop, click, click, click,
Down through the chimney with the good St. Nick."

At least, not until Andy turned the shower off and stepped out. Only then did she find, sitting on the counter next to her toothpaste and hairbrush, a brand-new Christmas card! The Stranger had sealed it in an envelope. With her name typed using the Crandall typewriter. The one with the imperfect "A".

Burning with curiosity, Andy pulled on her pajamas and plopped on the bed. She used a letter opener and sliced through the top seal before removing the card.

It was another one of those generic holiday cards, with its hackneyed pun and cartoonish illustration. *"Happy holly-days," said the wreath to the garland.* It was enough to make Andy groan as she opened it, spilling another *Whodunit* card onto the comforter.

The card featured another charmingly retro illustration, this one of a man, dressed as a burglar, climbing through a window. The caption said *The Prowler*. She studied it for a moment until... beep!

Her phone chimed with an incoming text message.

LIAM: HOW ARE YOU HOLDING UP?
ANDY: MY 2ND NIGHT IN XANADU ALCATRAZ!
LIAM: STAY THREE NIGHTS, GET ONE FREE!

That made her laugh.

ANDY: GOOD NIGHT.
LIAM: GOOD NIGHT, ANDY.

As she placed her phone on the nightstand, she found *something unusual,* having dropped behind a bedside photo of the Kenilworth Family. A single, long hair. It was not her own, which meant *someone else* had recently left it behind. In fact, there was only *one guest* at this party with hair of that color.

Amelia.

"The prowler," Andy said to herself, deep in thought.

Amelia had been in Andy's room.

Why?

CHAPTER SEVEN

Creeping out of her room in the middle of the night on Christmas Eve, Andy thought of Santa Claus. *Wouldn't that just be a hoot,* she thought, *if she stumbled across old Saint Nick himself, emptying his sack by the tree?* She savored the thought of the family greedily tearing into their gifts on Christmas morning, steaming cocoa in hand, and finding only giant lumps of dirty black coal.

She had to stifle her giggle. After all, she didn't want anyone to hear her stirring.

Not even a mouse.

She was on the case, and she knew no one would understand if they caught her sneaking about the house at this late hour.

The Christmas lights washed the quiet lodge in a warm glow, just enough for Andy to see that there was no Jackie sneaking a cookie from the kitchen. No Margaret in the study counting her pennies like a nouveau rich Scrooge. And, disappointedly, no Santa Claus tumbling down the chimney.

In fact, the only thing awake was a security camera, perched high above the foyer, with the little speckles of twinkle lights reflected in its wide-angle lens. Pivoting on its own, it scanned the entire space with each sweep. Part of the security system Liam had installed, Andy imagined what would happen if Margaret, alerted of movement on her computer, saw her slinking around on the monitor.

Go directly to jail.

Do not collect two hundred dollars.

Which was why Andy waited, at the base of the stairs, her back pressed against the wall. Watching and waiting. She had to make sure it didn't see her.

The camera turned in one direction. Then back again. Back and forth. Swiveling with an omnipotent eye, its red tally light glowered in the night like a nightmarish monster.

It pivoted. Andy counted.

Ten seconds.

So that's how long I have, she thought, as she prepared to make the run. Ten seconds to get down the hall and into the study before the camera would see her.

It pivoted.

It pivoted back.

It pivoted.

Andy ran.

Ten seconds. Her feet trod across the hardwood.

Eight seconds. Her slippers loosened. She realized if one fell off, it would be all the evidence Margaret would need. Forget the glass slipper from the fairy tales. Cotton and suede would do her in.

Six seconds. She was almost there.

Four seconds. Just a few more feet.

Two seconds. She dashed around the corner.

One second. The camera swung back.

It was as if Andy was never there. The slippers had stayed on.

Andy closed the door to the study behind her. Her heart was still racing. She made her way through the study's inner corridor and into the room. Reaching for her pocket, she pulled out her phone. Using its flashlight, it was time to investigate.

The home office looked pretty much as it did the previous day. The safe, its door once hidden behind a false display of books, was still ajar. That ancient desktop computer sat on the desk. The collection of antique typewriters was still on display. A Christmas tree glowed in the corner. Still, as she scanned the room, she couldn't shake the idea that she was missing something. No matter how trivial, there had to be *something* she'd overlooked. A clue who stole the diamond and set the calamitous events of the week in motion.

She stared at the desk, replaying the theft in her head.

Margaret had excused herself to the study. She opened the false façade hiding the safe, entered the combination, and placed the Diamond inside.

Andy stood there, in front of the now empty safe, when something occurred to her. How did the thief know Margaret's back would be turned at that exact moment? There was only one possible solution. The thief must have been watching her.

But from where?

Looking back towards the door and the small, transitional corridor leading into the study, Andy noticed a clear line of sight.

She crept into that narrow wood paneled passage and, crouching down, turned to face the desk and safe. She imagined someone hiding here, in the shadows, as Margaret placed the treasured Christmas Diamond into the safe. Still, how would the thief have gotten in without the camera, the one she'd spent her evening dodging, seeing them?

Then Andy remembered the card she'd gotten earlier in the evening. *The Prowler*, it had said. *What if someone was trying to help her?* If the other card had suggested Raphael, with its convenient rendering of a thief and food, could this card *also* contain some sort of allusion? *There was only way to find out,* she thought, reaching into her pocket. She pulled the card out and took another look. This illustration was of a burglar climbing through a window.

It couldn't be that simple.

Stepping back into the room, she fixed her gaze on the window.

Was it possible?

Andy walked over and opened the latch. She lifted the window and climbed out.

It was quite cold outside, and in the crisp air, the slushy layer of snow had frozen over. Andy was careful as she lowered herself from the window. She didn't want to disturb any evidence, assuming there were any. Her house slippers provided little insulation, and, as they touched down onto the ice, she felt the cold moisture almost immediately. She drew her pajamas tight against her thin frame, as if the thin fabric could protect her from the near-freezing temperature.

Scanning with her phone's light, something on the ground caught her attention. Directly under the window, which she'd been careful enough not to disturb, were a pair of shoe prints in the snow!

The distinctive tread pattern had maintained its shape, thanks to the ice crystals that had formed in the night. Andy grabbed her phone and took a snapshot. The thief had left behind a very incriminating clue!

Andy climbed back through the window, eager to get back into the warm lodge. Her mind drifted to the heated tile of her bathroom. She relished the thought of thawing her numb feet when she got back to her room.

But first she had a bigger problem. There was the sound of footsteps coming from the hallway! Someone else was awake! Being that Andy hadn't heard a clatter on the roof when she was outside, it was most likely *not* jolly ol' Saint Nick. Whoever it was, they were getting closer! Andy realized how it would look if she were spotted in the study at that hour. Considering her options, she knew she only had one.

She had to hide.

The door swung open, and it was Margaret who entered the room. She reached for the light switch, and turning it on, found the room was empty. There was no sign that anyone had been there, save for a few droplets of melted ice on the floor from where Andy had climbed in. Luckily, Margaret didn't notice them.

Margaret reached into the desk and retrieved a pair of reading glasses. Slamming the drawer shut, the woman stood still. Her head swiveled, her eyes searching, as if she possessed some sixth sense... *as if she knew someone else was in that room.* Luckily, she didn't think to check behind the Christmas tree, where Andy had tucked herself away. Margaret simply took the reading glasses and snapped the light off before leaving the room.

Alone once again, Andy sighed with relief.

THE TWO BUNNIES STRODE into the kitchen. Peering around with their giant black eyes, it was clear they were foraging for food. It had been hours since they were last fed, and their tiny tummies were rumbling hungrily. Their eyes landed upon a plate of Christmas cookies, fresh baked by Bridgette. How would these two rabbits go about pilfering these captivating confections, their moist dough still warm, covered in a brilliant red and green frosting?

Luckily for the two bunnies, they were only slippers. And the woman wearing them, one Jackie Evenson, possessed something that the terrycloth bunnies did not: opposable thumbs.

Before she could bite into her treat, Jackie heard scampering behind her! The sudden burst of energy startled her. Luckily, it wasn't one of the judgmental Kenilworths. It was Andy.

"Jackie!" her young protégé exclaimed in relief. It seemed she too was happy to see that the occupant of the kitchen was not one of her *less-adored* housemates.

"Andy!" Jackie exclaimed. "You scared the bejeezus out of me!" Then, she held up the plate of cookies, as if sharing the purloined pastries might ease some of the guilt. "Midnight snack?"

But Andy wasn't interested in sharing Jackie's ill-gotten goodies. She held up the card that was left during her shower.

Jackie studied the card and its art. "The Prowler?"

"At first, I didn't know what it meant," Andy explained. "But then, when I went into the study, I asked myself... how *did* the thief get in *without being seen*?"

Jackie's brain pondered the question. If there was one thing she liked more than a good old-fashioned cookie, it was a good old-fashioned mystery, and this one kept her on her toes. *Literally.*

"Look at this." Andy pointed to the photo she'd taken outside the window. "Footprints. Outside the study."

Jackie grinned. Andy had found a missing piece of the puzzle. "The window. That's how they got in?"

"And how they got away." Andy exclaimed. "If we can match the shoes, we could find the thief!"

Jackie took another look at Andy's prints. All they needed to do now was locate the pair of footwear that matched.

"Sounds like we've got a glass slipper to find."

LUCKILY FOR PRINCE Charming, he didn't have to deal with the likes of Margaret Kenilworth when he was trying to track down the mysterious owner of his glass slipper. As dreadful as Lady Tremaine and her daughters Drizella and Anastasia were, Andy figured Margaret, Gary, Leonora, and Amelia would have given them a run for their money. *Not even the Brothers Grimm, with their boundless, fantastical imaginations, could have conceived such dreadful characters*, she chuckled to herself as she climbed the lodge's sweeping stairs.

Making their way down the upstairs hallway towards the bedrooms, Andy and Jackie strode as quietly as possible, well aware their host would not appreciate that their late-night impromptu investigation.

"We shouldn't be up here," Jackie whispered. "If Margaret finds us..."

"You should see that bottle of melatonin in the bathroom." Andy sought to ease her concerns. "Nothing less than a reindeer stampede is going to wake that woman up."

"Who do we start with?" Jackie asked, enjoying the fact that, at least for the moment, the detective and sidekick had switched roles.

"There was *definitely* one person who was missing around the time of the blackout," Andy remembered. "I'd say it's time we finally find out *why*."

She held up a plastic baggie containing *the incriminating hair* that she'd found in her room. Jackie's eyes lit up with curiosity as another clue was revealed.

AMELIA VANDERKAMP HAD wondered why she bothered to accept Margaret's invitation. The rest of the Vanderkamp family had disembarked for the South Pacific and were spending their holiday on Banwa, their own private 15-acre island with its beachfront villas, one for each member of the family. The crystal-clear water of the Sulu Sea was warm and tranquil, and she imagined her sisters sitting on a beach, soaking up the warm rays of sunshine, while she lay in the guest bed of a cold, dark ski lodge. Worse, she watched as the object of her affections rebuffed her advances in favor of, of all people, a barista.

All she could do now was wait for Margaret to end the self-imposed house arrest and, with a few precious days left in the Christmas holiday, jet off to Manila to catch a connecting sea plane, and join her own family for what little time remained of their retreat.

For the time being, however, she slept.

The door to Amelia's room opened. Jackie crept up to Amelia's bedside, taking careful note of the heiress's obsession with pink. Psychologically speaking, the color had a calming effect. It was soft, healing, and peaceful. However, in Amelia's case, Jackie suspected a simpler, less thoughtful rationale behind the preponderance of that specific hue.

Immaturity.

"Amelia..." Jackie whispered to the sleeping heiress as she clung tight to her stuffed unicorn, which was, of course, pink.

Amelia's eyes opened, noticing Jackie standing at the foot of the four-post bed while Andy rifled through her luggage set. "What's going on? What are you doing here?"

"We wanted to ask you some questions." Jackie announced.

Amelia squinted at her watch and stared at her two guests in disbelief. "At two in the morning?" She then turned to Andy, who was going through her bags. "What are you looking for?"

"Your shoes." Andy stood, approaching the bed.

"*My* shoes?" Amelia was still half-asleep, both disoriented and in disbelief.

"You go for a walk the other night?" Andy asked.

"It's freezing out." Amelia scoffed, once again thinking of that warm tropical island.

"Where are your shoes, Amelia?" Jackie asked. She'd written enough interrogation scenes in her novels to know a dodge when she saw one.

"The closet," the heiress replied.

Andy turned her attention to the closet while Jackie kept her attention on their suspect, who, in her silk pajamas and tucked into the bed with her pink unicorn, couldn't look more like a spoiled little rich girl if she'd tried.

"Where were you when the blackout happened?" Jackie asked.

"Am *I* a suspect now?" Amelia scoffed.

"Everyone in this house is a suspect." Jackie replied matter-of-factly.

"Unless you have an alibi." Andy suggested.

Amelia groaned. *Hadn't they been through this? How many times would she have to tell the same story before these two would-be detectives would listen?* "I told you. I came back here to lie down. And then Liam came in."

Andy turned cold. "Yes, Liam told me all about it."

"He did?" Amelia was still in denial that her onetime boyfriend would find Andy more attractive than herself.

"Nothing happened between you two, did it?" Andy challenged her.

Amelia looked up at her. And Jackie. And she sighed. "Okay, so I might have... *embellished* a little earlier."

"Embellished how?" Jackie crossed her arms in an accusatory stance.

"You're right," Amelia sighed, staring at Andy. "Nothing happened."

"In fact, he told you he wanted you *to leave*, didn't he?" Andy challenged her.

"You're the detective, Jackie." Amelia said, turning to the woman she believed to be the alpha dog in this scenario. "Is that detail really relevant to my alibi?"

"Just answer her question," Jackie deflected.

Amelia knew she had little choice. The time had come to be truthful. She might as well stop thinking about the relationship that was in her past and start thinking about the island that was in her future.

"Yes." Amelia said before adding a curt follow-up. "Happy?"

"Not quite." It was Jackie's turn to speak up. "At what point did you go into Andy's room?"

Andy held up the hair she'd found before Jackie continued. "And if I were you, I'd think carefully about your answer."

Amelia sighed with a sentiment that was both rare and new for her. *Defeat*. "I saw the way Liam was laughing and flirting with her and I got jealous, okay?"

"Because he was laughing?" Jackie was confused.

"Because he never smiled at *me* that way," Amelia admitted.

"Really?" Andy hadn't, until now, ever felt special compared to *anyone*.

"I wanted to find out more about you," Amelia nodded. "I mean, what makes you, *a nobody from Maine...*"

"New Hampshire." Jackie replied.

"*Massachusetts*." Andy corrected, going through each of Amelia's shoes.

"...so *special*." Amelia continued. "Was it stupid? Yeah. Petty? Definitely. But no, I didn't take Margaret's Christmas Diamond."

Jackie looked at Andy, who had just finished going through Amelia's footwear. They ran the gamut from red bottomed Louboutins to a Sotheby's exclusive Louis Vuitton and Nike collaboration. None of it, however, matched Andy's photo.

"Well?" Jackie asked.

"She's telling the truth," Andy said. "The treads aren't even close. And they are way too small."

"Told you," Amelia scoffed, and then, in a rare moment of humanity, continued. "Look, I'm not here to cause trouble. I'm here because Margaret invited me. She led me to believe that I could win Liam back. But the minute I saw him with you, I knew that was impossible. I let her get into my head. And for that, I'm sorry. We're just not meant to be."

She and Andy locked eyes in a rare moment of mutual understanding and appreciation. Although Andy knew the sentiment was likely to fade before morning, it was enough for now. As she and Jackie left, it made her feel better.

At least until she remembered that there was still a jewel thief under their roof.

And that she was facing imminent arrest.

"You think it's going to be that easy?" Olivia asked, as she allowed Andy and Jackie access to her shoes in her bedroom. "Finding an incriminating shoe?"

"Nothing's that easy," Andy admitted. "But we're running out of time and ideas."

"I don't suppose they'd be any *other* reason for someone to be outside," Jackie asked, seeking to eliminate the obvious. "Groundskeeper? Some neighbor's kid hired to shovel the driveway?"

"No." Olivia agreed with Andy. "I don't suppose you've considered the possibility that there never *was* a theft."

"Go on." Andy sat with Jackie standing over her shoulder.

"Well, my mother was the *only one* in the study when the diamond was taken," Olivia said. "*And* my mother was the *only one* on the stairs when she fell."

Andy pondered this. While staging the theft of her Christmas Diamond as a pretense to subject her family to psychological warfare felt like something Margaret would be capable of, throwing herself down the stairs felt like a bridge too far. When she pointed out that fact, Olivia seemed to agree.

"Mother always did shy away from physical injury," Olivia noted. "She loved coming up here but never went skiing with the family. She never even went snorkeling when we all went to Grand Turk."

"She broke a nail once and you would have thought she'd broken a bone." Jackie chuckled, thinking of her friend's classic overreactions. Yes, the idea of the woman willfully taking a header down the stairs seemed outlandish, even by Margaret's standards.

"I guess you're right." Olivia finally said. "But that doesn't change the fact that you're asking my family to let you search their rooms a second time."

"A tall order?" Jackie asked, already knowing the answer.

"I think you'd have an easier time proving my mother threw herself down the stairs." Olivia said with a knowing grin.

"Actually," Andy said. "We may not have to."

She had an idea. And it was a tasty one.

BRIDGETTE ALWAYS ADORED Christmas morning. Growing up in Tottenham, one of five daughters of a bookkeeper and a bank clerk, December 25th had been a magical time in the Ratcliffe household. There were pantomime shows at the New Victoria Theater; Christmas crackers filled with prizes; the Queen's annual Christmas address, which Bridgette adored; and, last but not least, the stockings that hung from the foot of her and her siblings' beds, awaiting a late-night visit from Father Christmas. Most memorable, however, was the food. Yorkshire pudding filled with bisto, Christmas fruit cake covered with marzipan and icing, mince pies, brandy butter, mulled wine, the list went on and on.

This was why, when Andy came to her bright and early on the morning of the 25th, with the idea of a good old-fashioned Christmas feast, Bridgette sparked to the idea. She thought it was odd that Andy specified she wanted to something to *"keep the family preoccupied,"* but Bridgette agreed it would be a good way to end the troubled holiday on a high note. While no one would celebrate a partridge in the pear tree, she could at least make sure she stuffed their stomachs with Christmas joy.

Not even Raphael would have attempted such an ambitious Christmas spread. Bridgette recreated all of the traditional favorites she'd grown up with, which included plates of beef and mutton with currants, raisins, prunes, spices and wine. She even threw in some of the American classics as well: red and green Christmas pancakes, ham with pineapple, and, of course, turkey. Luckily, Raphael had kept the pantry well-stocked.

As the scent of this delightful spread filled the lodge from top to bottom, the family filed into the dining room with hungry curiosity.

"Something smells amazing!" Liam exclaimed.

"Did Raphael come back?" asked a suspicious Olivia.

"Unfortunately, not," Bridgette announced as she entered with one last plate of pancakes for the center of the table. "Happy Christmas everyone! Please gather 'round! I hope you've brought your appetites."

After spending the last couple of days as Margaret's captive guests, the feast provided a welcome respite for those rumbling tummies. By now, they'd grown tired of sandwiches and microwaved leftovers from Raphael's previous dinner. In fact, they were so distracted by the morning banquet, no one noticed that someone, the quietest and meekest among them, was missing. At least, *not at first*.

"Where is Candace?" Margaret addressed the elephant *not* in the room.

"She said had something to take care of," Bridgette notified her, "but suggested we all get started."

"Maybe I should go have a look," Margaret suggested, lifting herself from her seat. "You know she has a knack for causing trouble."

"Oh, sit down, Margaret." Jackie had heard enough. "Leave the poor girl alone. If Bridgette said she'll be here; I believe she'll be here."

Margaret sat back down. If there was one person who could put the woman in her place, it was her trusted friend.

Indeed, while the family gorged themselves on Bridgette's edible distractions, Andy put her plan, *her true plan*, into motion. If the goal had been to make sure the rooms were empty and available to be searched, then it was a rousing success. Sneaking down the hallway, Andy listened to the conversations from below, confirming that every voice was accounted for. There was Gary's entitled boastfulness, Leonora's arrogance, Harper's sheltered naivete, Amelia's shameless pandering, Olivia's innocence and, above all, Margaret's dominating pomposity. Andy had even thought she overheard Liam bet someone that his Aunt Leonora would disapprove of the breakfast. Bridgette explained to each of the guests the origins of some of her more regional specialties. For a moment, Andy missed the French accent of Raphael, who undoubtedly would have engaged Leonora in one of his memorable rants.

Having the entire second floor of the lodge to herself, Andy went from room to room, on the hunt for her elusive glass slipper: the shoe that matched the tread from the prints found outside. It was like looking for the proverbial needle in a haystack, especially when one considered how many pairs of shoes some of these people owned.

Andy searched every room, even Bridgette's, although she hadn't expected the butler's meager wardrobe to yield anything of note. Margaret's own collection was, like much of her possessions, a sizable and well-curated assortment of footwear, about four seasons out of style. Gary and Leonora's designer Italian leather winter wear turned out to be slightly off-center samples of Times Square's finest. Liam, far from a fashionista, had the least daunting selection, comprising two pairs of dress shoes, one pair of winter boots, and six variations on the same sneaker. Olivia had a much larger assortment, some of which being her own design, but her feet were at least four sizes too small. In fact, the *only* interesting thing Andy found during her search was Gary's Santa suit, which was left abandoned on the floor of a closet. The outfit was ordained to be untouched for the next three hundred sixty-three days.

Having finished her search, Andy marched downstairs. She found the family gathered in the dining room, sitting around the table, and partaking in Bridgette's feast as expected. Margaret, in her usual haughty tone, looked up. "There you are. We were worrying you wouldn't join us."

Jackie, who knew a ruse when she saw one, knew what Andy had been up to. She didn't even have to say anything. She was more than capable of communicating her curiosity with a simple glance. And, judging from the look Andy gave her in return, her protégé was onto *something.*

That's when Margaret leaned over to Andy with a conceited grin. "I suggest you eat something, Candace. I don't know how often they feed people down at the jail."

Andy threw down her gauntlet. "Why don't you give the Detective a call and invite him to join us? Then you could ask him yourself."

"And why would I do that?" Margaret asked, bristling at Andy's temerity.

"Because *I* know who stole the Christmas Diamond," Andy announced. "And it wasn't Raphael."

CHAPTER EIGHT

Detective Billings thought he was finished with the Kenilworths for the holidays. He had someone in custody for both the suspected assault on Margaret and the attempted theft of her beloved Christmas Diamond. Yet, sure enough, on Christmas morning, he got a hasty call from the old woman, demanding his presence yet again.

Margaret felt convinced that Andy was about to hang herself, and she wanted to make sure she handed the girl enough rope to do so. *Especially* if it would prove, once and for all, she was right about her daughter's friend. For a moment on that cold winter morning, Detective Billings had considered *declining* the invitation, but he knew any conversation regarding the blatant disregard of boundaries would fall upon deaf ears.

By the time the Detective arrived at the Kenilworth home for the third time that week, it was nearly noon. Bridgette had cleared her breakfast from the dining room and the family awaited the Detective's arrival in the study. Despite the Christmas music bellowing from Margaret's phonograph, the presents still sat untouched under the tree. The family had been too preoccupied with either to get into the Christmas spirit. However, as they would soon discover, their Christmas wouldn't be *completely* without gifts.

"If you would, please join me in the dining room," Andy announced as the Detective made his way into the home.

Sure enough, as the family gathered around the long table, there were Christmas cards laid out in front of their seats. Each had their names on it, typed with the same Crandall typewriter that had bestowed Andy's cards upon her. Jackie chuckled. Her spunky young fan had a sense of humor, and she found the thought refreshing. Especially given her current company.

"Please have a seat and be sure to sit where your card is." Andy told the family as they shuffled in and took their seats. Detective Billings, content with being the proverbial fly on the wall, stood at the rear of the room.

"Now that you're all here," Andy said, "you're probably wondering what all this is about.

Well, I thought since we all had *so* much fun playing Margaret's little game the other night... I'd bring us together for a brand new one! And this one is called... *To Catch a Thief*!"

The family grumbled. These continued theatrics had worn on them.

"Oh, come on, just come out with it." Gary exclaimed.

"Where's your sense of fun?" Liam asked.

"By now? Back in New York." Gary answered, shooting his sister an angry glance. "And with any luck, I'll be along soon enough."

"Before we begin," Andy said. "Please open your cards. Just don't show anyone what yours says."

One by one, the family members did as she asked and opened their cards. Just like the ones that Andy received, each of them had been given a game card from the *Whodunit* board game in their envelopes. Something personal. Something that shook each of them. It seemed only Detective Billings was spared the indignity.

"Please," Andy reminded each of them. "Don't show anyone which card you have."

However, that was the *last* thing on their mind. In fact, most of the guests' respective reactions to the ignominious cards felt more like embarrassment.

"Shall we begin?" Andy continued before turning to Jackie. "Jackie, let's start with you."

Jackie flipped her card over. "The Detective."

"Easy one." Andy smiled. "Olivia?

Olivia turned her card around. *The Innocent.*

Harper laughed. "Bor-ring."

"We'll just overlook that time you stole that candy bar from the camp cafeteria." Andy laughed to Olivia before turning to Liam. "Liam? *I bet* I know what yours says."

Liam revealed his card around for all to see. *The Gambler.*

"Appropriate," Gary muttered under his breath.

"And speaking of Liam," Andy then turned to her romantic rival. "Amelia?"

Amelia turned hers around. *The Narcissist.*

"I hope there's a point to all this," Margaret grumbled.

"Actually," Andy proclaimed. "*This* is where it gets interesting. Let's go back to the night the diamond was taken. Everyone went to the great room after dinner for post-dinner cocktails and hot chocolate. Everyone, except for Gary, who'd snuck away to change his clothes and returned dressed as Santa. Around 7:15, Bridgette tripped, spilling the tray of cocoa on Leonora. That's when Leonora insisted she be fired, and Margaret subjected her to a rather public humiliation."

"And *well deserved*, if you ask me," Leonora sneered.

"More on that in a bit," Andy replied before continuing her story. "7:20pm. Harper went to the kitchen, where she stole an alcoholic beverage."

"I'm sorry, she did *what*?!" Gary exclaimed in surprise.

"But that's not as surprising as what happened next," Andy continued. "Harper and her mother stepped into the foyer to fight. Not about the drink, but about college."

"What *about* college?" Gary asked, beginning to piece everything together.

"Harper," Andy turned to the youngest among them. "Please share *your* card with everyone?"

Harper did just that. Her card, tellingly, was *The Liar.*

"It would seem," Andy turned to Gary. "That your daughter's interest in going overseas has little to do with the studying she's no longer doing, and more to do with a young man named Cedric."

"You dropped out?" Gary shouted, "Again?"

"Dad…" Harper started, her level of shame building.

"What about the tuition checks I've been sending?" Gary asked, reaching for the truth.

"They're subsidizing her lifestyle as an *influencer*." Andy revealed, much to Harper's shame. "So, while she may *seem* to have no motivation for taking the diamond, what you might *not* know is that Margaret had threatened to cut off her trust fund for dating, what was it she called him? *A commoner*?"

Gary turned to his sister, aghast. "You knew about this?!"

"I was simply looking out for her best interest!" Margaret explained. "How did you know?"

"Because his own text admitted he'd never been to Paris," Andy replied. "I doubt that would be the case if he was coming from a family as superciliously privileged as this one."

"Thank you." Leonora said, missing the insult.

"Stealing the diamond would allow Harper to eat her Cedric cake and keep her rich lifestyle, too." Andy continued.

"But I was outside the whole time! I didn't take it!" Harper insisted.

"That is true," Andy admitted. "You didn't. But when you mentioned your aunt's reaction to the news about Cedric, it touched a nerve, didn't it, Jackie?"

Jackie remembered their interrogation of the young girl, and how there seemed to be more to the story than they were aware. "It did."

But Margaret had heard enough. "This is preposterous!"

"If that's the case," Andy turned to the host. "I assume you wouldn't mind sharing *your* card with the table?"

Turning red, either from shame, anger, or some combination of the two, Margaret flipped her card over. *The Lover*. That earned a childish giggle from her brother, Gary.

"I propose," Andy accused, "that the reason Harper's relationship rubbed you the wrong way... was because *you yourself had been through the same thing*!"

"Easy..." warned Margaret through gritted teeth.

"Everyone's noticed the lack of familial resemblance between Liam and Olivia." Andy recalled Olivia's own offhanded remark: *No one believed we were actually related*. "Is it possible that's because Liam's father wasn't *actually* Mr. Kenilworth?"

"Wait, *what*?" Olivia cried out. Clearly, this revelation was news to at least *one* of Margaret's children.

"You fell in love with someone your mother felt was beneath you, didn't you?" Andy pointed to Margaret. "That would explain why you demanded Harper end her relationship. Because *your* mother made you do the same thing. Let me guess... Liam's father wasn't quite *good enough* for dear old mom?"

You could have heard a pin drop at that moment. Not only had the family history been shattered, but it had been by the *last* person Margaret would have expected. However, Jackie knew that this was one trait of a good detective. *Never see them coming*, she always said.

Now that Andy had connected the dots for the guests, they thought back to game night, to something Margaret had said.

Something that felt off handed at the time suddenly made a lot more sense. *In the spirit of the season,* Margaret had said to Harper, *allow me to give you some advice for your Christmas stocking. Never forget your place.* It turned out the advice had been even *more* personal than they could have imagined.

"That is the most absurd thing I have ever heard!" Margaret deflected.

"It's true." Liam spoke up.

"Wait, you *knew*?" Olivia demanded of her brother.

"The letter you got in the mail," Andy remembered back to that day she arrived and the mail that Olivia found on the table. "From the genealogy company."

"I'd always suspected." Liam confirmed. "Now I had confirmation."

"You should have told me!" Olivia protested.

Liam defended himself. "In case you hadn't noticed, there's been a lot going on these past couple of days!"

"Allow me to continue," Andy drew attention back to the task at hand. "At 7:40, Margaret went to return the necklace to her safe, while I left the room to make coffee. But when I was gone, the blackout happened."

The family murmured amongst each other. Remembering what had happened. How Olivia had panicked, revealing a fear of the dark. How Gary chided his sister in absentia about the power bill. Then, what had happened next...

"As everyone reacted," Andy continued, remembering the answers the family had provided during their questioning. "Gary left the room to take off his Santa suit."

"And to find the breakers," Gary reminded them, before adding: "No one *else* was going to do it."

"As I recall, *I* was going to do it." Liam spoke up in his own defense.

"Right," his uncle scoffed. "You didn't even know where they were!"

"Like *you* did?" Liam shot back.

"As I recall, *I* was the one who found them," Gary boasted.

"Are you two children finished?" Olivia interrupted them. "Because I'd like to hear the rest of what she has to say."

"Whatever," Gary shut down, as he often did when losing an argument, and crossed his arms. Exactly what a spoiled, petulant child might do.

"*However*," Andy continued, "when Liam went upstairs, instead of looking for the breaker box, he confronted Amelia, who, by that point, had returned to her room."

"That's true." Liam admitted, exchanging a glance with Amelia.

"In any case," Andy pointed out, "neither she nor Liam would have had time to steal the diamond."

"Exactly." Amelia spoke up. "It seems these little theatrics of yours are just a waste of my time."

However, as the heiress went to stand, Margaret snapped. "Oh, sit down, you spoiled little brat. If I'm going to have to listen to this nonsense, we *all* will."

"Please, Andy," Jackie grinned. "Continue with this... *nonsense*."

"In that case," Andy resumed without missing a beat. "We're left with two questions. *Who* cut the power? And *who* stole the necklace? We're all assuming someone just went to the breaker box and threw the switch. But as I've just established, *everyone* has an alibi during that time."

"Everyone *except her*," Amelia said, casting a look at Margaret. Having lost Liam, there was no longer a reason to keep up her charade. She detested Margaret.

"Yes," Andy admitted, "and while it *is* tempting to suspect that Margaret staged the entire incident *and* threw herself down the stairs as some twisted Machiavellian form of psychological warfare... it's excessive. Even by *her* standards."

"Thank you," Margaret said.

"But what if someone didn't just go to the breaker box and flip a switch?" Andy asked. "What if the blackout was the *culmination* of something set in motion hours before?"

That got everyone thinking. Was it possible that they'd all been thinking about this so incorrectly? Was the answer so clever as to be beyond their comprehension?

"Gary," Andy turned to him. "You hang the Christmas lights outside this lodge every year?"

"Yes," he replied, taking pride in his artistic work.

"And you admitted having blown a fuse in the past," she followed up, remembering his own words during their questioning. *I'm in charge of the Christmas lights every year. Believe me, I know a thing or two about fuses.*

"Yes," he confirmed.

"And, as Raphael admitted," she thought back again. "The wiring in the lodge is so old that sometimes even the appliances are a problem!" She remembered Raphael telling Detective Billings in his mangled English, *Is older house. Older wiring. I have to be careful with the appliances as it is.*

"Therefore," Andy kept focused on Gary as she went in for the proverbial kill. "Is it *possible* you overloaded the circuits so *precisely* that the flip of *one switch* would have tripped the circuit breaker?"

He just laughed. "And how in the world do you propose I could have possibly done such a thing?"

"Easy," Andy replied. "You simply bought your sister a very expensive Italian espresso machine with a considerable demand for electric power. Then you specifically requested that I use that device at the *exact moment* you needed the breaker tripped."

Everyone thought back. Indeed, Gary *was* the one who suggested: *How about we have the professional make some coffee? I, for one, would love an espresso.*

"Okay, so assuming that I somehow tripped *the breaker*," Gary challenged Andy, "Then what?"

"You used the search for the circuit breaker to explain your absence during the theft of the diamond." Andy noted.

"Except, how would I *possibly* have time to do that and search for the circuit breaker at the same time?"

"Easy," Andy replied. "You didn't *have* to search. Because you already knew where the circuit breaker was. After all, you *are* in charge of the Christmas lights every year, right? And know a thing or two about fuses?"

He squirmed, hearing his *own* testimony twisted and used against him. "How does that explain the boots?"

Andy just looked at him, allowing him to continue.

"You were looking for the boots to match the prints you saw outside the window, right? The window *you* claim the thief used to sneak into the study? I know you were searching the rooms while Bridgette was serving her haggis, or whatever that was."

"Roasted pheasant." Bridgette clarified.

"I was, yes," Andy admitted.

"And I'm assuming you went through my luggage," Gary lobbed another accusation.

"I did." Andy admitted again.

"Did you find *anything* in my possession to match those prints?" he challenged. "No, you didn't. And do you know *why* you didn't? Because I didn't make them!"

"You're right," Andy acknowledged, exchanging a glance with a nervous Jackie, who feared that her protégé had been outsmarted by the family ne'r do well. "There was no pair of boots in your possessions that matched."

"Thank you," Gary nodded, feeling proud of himself.

"But there was a pair of boots," Andy shot back, resuming her hunt. Gary turned back to her, again growing nervous. "And they were *right under our nose* the whole time!"

Reaching down, she placed a pair of black boots on the table for all to see. The room erupted in excited murmuring as everyone realized what they were.

"Santa boots." Andy clarified. Everyone was present when Gary had entered the party in his Santa costume, which, notably, included *those same boots*. Which she'd found tossed aside with the rest of the Santa costume.

"He'd already cased the study earlier," Andy suggested, remembering back to the intruder she'd heard outside her window while getting settled. "*That* was the noise I heard outside my window earlier, since it's right underneath."

"You're not seriously buying any of this, are you?" Gary asked his fellow guests. Such a question at this point was rhetorical, however, as the answer was an unequivocal yes.

"So, he'd figured out how to get in," Andy continued. "Past the locked door to steal the diamond. All he needed was to cut the power which I did on his behalf when I tried to use the coffee machine."

"And why would I *need* my older sister's diamond?" Gary scoffed.

Andy turned to both Gary and his wife. "Gary and Leonora, perhaps your cards could help enlighten us?"

Leonora revealed her card, pretending to be puzzled. "The Charlatan?"

"Margaret," Andy turned to her host. "Your brother and his wife claimed they wanted you to double down and invest your returns, but you told them you wanted to *pull* your investments. Isn't *that* the reason they were so upset the day I arrived?"

"Yes," Margaret nodded.

"Which would have caused their Ponzi scheme to collapse," Andy noted. "But that's not *why* you cashed out, is it? After all, as you said, you were making excellent returns... even if you were the only one involved in their pyramid scheme to do so. No. The truth is... the financial situation isn't quite the *entire story*, is it?"

Olivia looked over and read Gary's card aloud. "The Philanderer."

"Your sister knew about your affair." Andy asked Gary, as the room erupted in shocked gasps.

"What affair?" Harper shot her father.

Andy then turned to Bridgette. "Bridgette, your card?

She turned it over and showed it to everyone. *The Harlot.*

"With *the maid*?" Harper gasped.

"Butler," Bridgette corrected her.

"An unstable marriage would have made any investment in their partnership particularly risky, wouldn't it? Especially since, in a divorce, Leonora would have been entitled to *half* their assets, cutting Margaret's share from one *half*... to one *quarter*." Andy asked Margaret, before turning her attention once again to Bridgette. "And let's be honest, no *experienced butler* would have made so clumsy a spill unless, of course, it was on purpose. Jealousy of a *particular and vengeful spouse*, perhaps?"

Bridgette lowered her head. "It wasn't fair."

"You witch!" Leonora exclaimed.

"He deserved better!" Bridgette defended herself.

"Better than what, the help?!" Leonora asked, boiling in outrage.

"He realized he would not get away cleanly with the diamond," Andy stuck to the task at hand, solving the mystery. "So, aware that his sister was already suspicious of me, he stashed it in my things when we split up to search the rooms. But that still left a problem, didn't it? You needed money to pay back your other investors. So, when you *couldn't* get the diamond, you decided that you'd have to get your money differently, didn't you? *Inheritance.*"

"You're accusing me of throwing my own sister down the stairs?" Gary scoffed.

"Throw, no." Andy stated. "It had to look like *an accident*. Which you'd set up in advance, just like you did with the coffee machine." She imagined Gary setting up a tripwire. Then, knowing he'd sabotaged the stairs, he'd called out as he reached for that antique firearm: *Margaret, check upstairs. I'm going out back!*

"All you had to do," Andy continued. "Was wait for her to come back down and trip! After, of course, you turned off the cameras."

Horrified, Margaret turned to her brother. "Gary? Is that true?"

But Andy wasn't about to let up. "Correct me if I'm wrong, Gary, but if something happens to her, you're the only one in this room who instantly gets four zeroes added to their net worth."

Gary sat as his sister shook her head in disdain. "After everything I've done for you?!"

Andy then turned to Detective Billings. "Your move, Detective."

As Detective Billings turned towards him, Gary shoved himself back from the table and leapt to his feet. Then, turning to the hallway, he made a run for the lodge's front door. The Detective, knowing he wouldn't get far, grabbed his radio. "He's coming your way."

THERE WERE *many* reasons that this year's annual Kenilworth Christmas Gathering would live long in infamy. A jewel heist. Assault and battery. Many threats. Even the inadvertent theft of one little drummer boy figurine. But none of them compared to the image of Gary and Leonora, the black sheep in a family that was full of them, being loaded into a waiting police cruiser on Christmas morning. At that point, not even their own daughter, only days away from embarking on a potential life-changing journey to France with the love of her life, could muster any sympathy. Margaret, who ordinarily would have cherished an opportunity to win a pyrrhic victory against her brother, found herself both disgusted and disappointed. Bridgette, aware of her own past transgressions, felt sad. She couldn't believe that Gary, *her* Gary, was capable of such diabolical acts. There was, however, at least one silver lining for the ambitious home wrecking butler. Raphael, one of her only friends, returned to the house. After all, Gary's guilt now exonerated the Gallic gourmand.

The family watched in horrified amusement as the cruisers pulled away with Gary and Leonora shoved in the back, on their way to spend the rest of their Christmas day, if not *many* Christmas days to come, as guests of the California penal system. *Perhaps they'd need someone to play Santa on game night as well*, Andy imagined, chuckling to herself.

The real-life crime reality show having ended, Olivia turned to go back inside the house. Her mother, however, held out a hand to stop her.

"Wait," Margaret said to her daughter as she stopped and turned. "Can we talk for a second?"

"That's funny," Olivia scoffed. "I can't imagine what else there is to say at this point."

"I know," Margaret replied. "I'm so sorry I never shared the truth with you. But you have to know, everything I've done, all the sacrifices I've made, I don't regret any of it. Not only that, but I'd do it all again. Because all I care about, all I've ever cared about, is giving you a good life. To set you up for success."

The older woman wiped away a tear, which touched her daughter. After all, she couldn't remember the last time, if ever, her mother had displayed anything resembling an honest emotion.

"I know I can be overbearing," Margaret continued. "But it was always from a place of love. And look at you! You're independent. With a good job. A place of your own. I must have done *something* right."

Olivia found herself speechless at her mother's sincerity. The only response she could even think of in the moment was a hug. Which is exactly what she did. For the first time in a long time, she hugged her mother, who returned the affection with a tight, warm embrace. It was a momentous instance of maternal love that touched everyone in the family, everyone that is, except the two people that were presently incarcerated.

As mother and daughter walked inside, hand in hand and possibly even heart in heart, Andy turned to Jackie. "So... did I make a pretty good sidekick?"

"Actually?" the writer replied. "I think you make an even *better* detective."

"Thanks to you." Andy smiled.

"You're the one who cracked the case." Jackie pointed out.

"But *you're* the one who sent the cards, *Detective*." Andy noted.

Jackie just smiled. She was waiting for Andy to realize that it was *she* who'd given her younger counterpart's investigation a little boost here and there. "All I did was give you a little nudge."

"Either way, thank you," Andy said.

"Speaking of, I've been thinking of writing a book about the past couple of days." Jackie told her.

"Oh?"

"Care to co-write it with me?" Jackie suggested.

The idea alone was enough to excite the aspiring writer. The opportunity to co-write a book with the very author who inspired her was almost too much to fathom. "Really?"

"I even have a title," Jackie continued, her eyes twinkling with creative inspiration. *Christmas Diamonds Are Forever*!

She could tell that Andy was not a fan, even if she refused to admit it. "Uh," was all the young woman could muster.

"*How the Thief Stole Christmas*?" suggested Jackie.

Better, Andy thought. But then she made a suggestion of her own. "How about just... *The Case of the Christmas Diamond*?"

Jackie grinned. It was perfect. In fact; she had only one further contribution. "Written by Jackie Evenson and Candace Kayne. A *Candy Cane* mystery!"

Andy hesitated again. "Not sure about that last part..."

Then, Andy noticed Liam going inside alone. He looked up and shot her a smile. Andy turned to Jackie. "I don't know about you, but I need a drink."

Jackie, who knew *exactly* why Andy wanted to go inside, was more concerned with making sure the two had the room to themselves. "You go on ahead," she said with that warm Jackie smile. "I'm going to see if I can't rustle me up some milk and cookies."

ANDY STEPPED INTO THE house, which was, for the first time since her arrival, uncharacteristically quiet. Given everything she'd been through, it surprised her to miss the excitement that seemed to follow the Kenilworth family wherever they roamed. The Annual Kenilworth Christmas Gathering, as Olivia initially christened it, had turned out to be many things, but dull was not one of them.

The family had set the Great Room for a Christmas soiree that would never come. Music that would never be played, pastries that would never be enjoyed, and a pile of presents that wouldn't be opened. Andy wondered what the protocol was for the gifts addressed to Gary and Leonora. *Perhaps a nice charity could find a use for them,* Andy thought. Ironic, given that the two might have been the *least* charitable people she knew.

Upon stepping into the Great Room, Andy happened upon Liam, who'd been helping himself to a familiar-looking beverage.

"That wouldn't be the Kenilworth's famous spiced ale, would it?" she asked with a knowing smile.

"I doubt it will stay fresh until the next Tibb's Eve."

"Then we'd better enjoy it while we can." Andy smiled.

The two poured their ales and then Andy raised her glass in a toast. "To the unceremonious end of another year's Kenilworth Christmas Gathering."

"May we never *ever* go through that again," Liam contributed.

Andy laughed. She might even have spurted some of the ale out of her nose, the way she had with a soda at summer camp all those years ago. The moment gave both Andy and Liam the cathartic release they so desperately needed.

"I'd say that was well earned," he said, finishing his glass. Then, placing it down, sincerity took hold of his handsome features. He *actually* had something serious to say. "About the other night. I never told you why I really went upstairs."

"It wasn't to look for the circuit breaker or confront Amelia?" Andy asked.

"It's my mother's lodge," he admitted. "You really don't think I know where the circuit breaker is?"

"What *were* you doing?"

"I was thinking about those Polaroids you and Olivia took back at camp," he told her. "I thought it would be a pleasant surprise if I, you know..."

Then, going under the tree, he retrieved a wrapped gift. The handwritten label read: *From Liam to Andy*. With a smile, he placed the present in Andy's hands. "Merry Christmas."

She hadn't expected this, nor did she expect to be as touched by the gesture as she was. However, being that it was likely to be her only Christmas present that year, she relished in the moment.

"Guess I'd better open it, huh?" she asked, trying not to sound too eager or excited.

"If you don't, I will," he grinned. It was difficult to tell which of the two was more excited by the gift. Finally, Andy tore into the paper; her raging curiosity having gotten the best of her.

Inside was a homemade photo album. Just as Liam had said, he filled it with Olivia's polaroids from their past. A chronicle of two childhood sweethearts who had no clue what adventures would lie ahead. It was enough to make Andy blush.

"Andy, I know I'm not perfect," he said. "But I also want you to know that whatever might lie ahead, I couldn't dream of another holiday without you."

"I don't know, maybe we'd better celebrate New Year's at my place," she said with a laugh. "You know, just in case?"

"But first, we have some business to tend to."

Her eyes narrowed, wondering where this was going. "Do we, now?"

Liam nodded and pointed upward. A sprig of mistletoe hung above them. "We couldn't *possibly* neglect a cherished, longstanding tradition."

Andy leaned in with a smile. "Merry Christmas."

Liam leaned in even further. "Merry Christmas."

Their lips touched. As their passion caught fire, the air between them became charged with the feelings of longing, anticipation and, ultimately, *connection*.

And *that* was how Andy would forever remember that Christmas holiday: as the day that she and Liam shared their first kiss.

Well, to be fair, there were a few *other things* as well, but none were as memorable or as epic as that.

About the Author

Peter Sullivan was born in Shrewsbury, Massachusetts and graduated from New York University's Tisch School of the Arts with a degree in Film and Television. After making the move to Los Angeles, he worked his way up the development ranks at Paramount, Artisan Television, and Hearst Entertainment. Since becoming Vice President of the production company Hybrid LLC in 2007, Sullivan has co-produced over 100 films. In addition to producing and writing, Sullivan has directed forty films himself, including "SECRET OBSESSION," which, with over 40 million viewers in its first 28 days, was one of the top 10 most viewed Netflix Originals ever; and the romantic comedy "CHRISTMAS UNDER WRAPS," which remains the highest rated program in Hallmark Channel history. In 2022, he directed the first original movie for Amazon's Freevee platform, "LOVE ACCIDENTALLY," starring Brenda Song and Denise Richards.

Some of his other notable works include the Netflix original feature "FATAL AFFAIR," starring Nia Long and Omar Epps; the Lionsgate release "THE SANDMAN," executive produced by Stan Lee and starring Tobin Bell from the "Saw" franchise; the Sony Pictures release "OMINOUS," starring Barry Watson; and Universal Pictures' "CUCUY: THE BOOGEYMAN" with Marisol Nichols and Brian Krause.

Severely hard of hearing since birth, Sullivan has recognized a need to provide a platform for filmmakers and artists with disabilities. In addition to teaching screenwriting at Culver City High School, he is also teaching masterclasses on writing and direction with Stage 32.